THE DEMON OF ELDERSTAY

Book One of The New Dark Saga

I. Ribbon

Praise for The Demon of Elderstay

"If you're into witty gnomes that embark on dangerous journeys, you have to give this book a try. If you're not into that, you still have to give it a try."

Eefje Kamps

"I laughed, I cried, and I devoured an entire box of chocolates as I contemplated what to do with my life until the next book in the series is released. I've recommended this book to everyone I meet, hoping to share my latest literary obsession and the excitement of anticipating the next books together."

Krista Gordon

"I would like to complain about the lack of sleep this book caused me. I turned the light out at 2:30AM. Was hopeless at pickleball the next day."

Kathy Hyde

"A wonderful adventure filled with magic, fantasy creatures, and dark elements."

Georgios Atsalis

"I. Ribbon's writing style is remarkable, the words they used throughout these pages felt warm and inviting but so marvellously descriptive. I am eager, nearly aching, for book two in *The New Dark Saga*."

Hailey Renee Jones

"A *huge* story packed into a modest package – pun absolutely intended. If you want adventure, danger, deliciously crude humour, and an unlikely hero, look no further."

Mackenzie Allquist

"If you're looking for a main character who perfectly melds a gay best friend vibe and the blundering heroics of *Hitchhikers Guide to the Galaxy's* Arthur Dent, you'll enjoy this fast-paced plot that leaves you wanting the next instalment of Gerome the Gnome."

Amanda Vaughn

"The characters are compelling and the world-building is rich with detail, making it easy to get lost in the story. Each page is full of unexpected twists that keep you on the edge of your seat. This novel is a must-read for anyone who loves a good fantasy adventure."

Kathryn Vakavosaki

"Witty and hilarious banter; Gerome the Gnome and his resident demon will have you clutching your sides in laughter."

Miranda Griffith

"An amazing cast of characters takes us on a quest filled with magic, intrigue, humour, and high stakes."

Sheree Parsons

"This was such a fun story. I loved the way the story unfolded and the characters reminded me of a *DnD* game with hilarious friends that just goes off the rails."

John Clarke

"*The Demon of Elderstay* is a fantasy of epic proportions that somehow manages to fit comfortably inside a Cracker Jack box (if the Cracker Jack box was about 200 pages)."

Jeni King

"I. Ribbon has captured that classic vibe of, 'these are the last people you would want to save the world, but there is no one else… so good luck.'"

Kate Haley

"I just loved everything about this story, the extremely relatable characters to the impressive world building. I'm excited to see further developments!"

Ashley Rathborne

"Ironic and thought-provoking at the same time."

Elena Piccioni

"A queer gnome possessed by a demon go on an adventure? Count me in! Such a witty and fun read. Can't wait to see what's next!"

Krystle Dullas

"*The Demon of Elderstay* is a fantasy adventure that will have you laughing one second, crying the next, and then wondering WTF just happened. I cannot wait for the next book!"

Casey Barnes

"I was chuckling as early as the prologue."

Emily Allain

"Gerome the gnome is plucky, witty, and effortlessly funny. In addition to masterful writing, the story challenges the reader to consider larger issues such as prejudice, greed, altruism, and addiction. With fondness, this story will always remain wedged in my own secret nine by nine cell within my heart."

Terra Hansing

"A perfect quick read in between the ginormous fantasy books I keep voluntarily burdening myself with. This book is cute AF in a dark humour kind of way."

Erika Karr

"I got fully lost in this story, and couldn't keep my eyes off the page near the end as Gerome has some difficult choices to make. The action is fast paced and it is clear how much care and love has gone into this book."

Elizabeth Hellier

"A hilarious must read for any fans of *DnD* and *The Hobbit*. I came for the fantasy and stayed for the sassiness!"

Caitlin Guardino

"It was such a fun read and I loveeeee Gerome. He is such a good egg. We must protect him at all costs!"

Jasmine Sperring

About the Author

Ira Ribbon is the New Zealand based author of the humorous fantasy series *The New Dark Saga*. She shares her life with her tolerant husband, a neurotic rescue dog, and a labour-intensive vegetable patch which demands as much attention as the aforementioned. She enjoys writing stories about a gnome fire mage burdened with demon, and wiling away the weekend arguing with her brother about the pronunciation of fantasy places.

Book Cover by Marco Staines

Illustrations by Maxime Desmettre and Carson Lowmiller

ISBN 978-1-0670086-0-4 (Paperback)
ISBN 978-1-0670086-2-8 (Hardcover)
ISBN 978-1-0670086-1-1 (eBook)

This book was 100% human made. I have no one to blame but myself.

To our inner demons. Yours and mine.

Without them, we'd never find our light.

Acknowledgements

A heartfelt thank you to everyone who has helped me forcefully yank Gerome from the depths of my imagination onto page. To my husband, Chris, for this unwavering support and encouragement throughout this journey. To Clare, Dee, Hayden, Richard, and Robert, my long-standing D&D group, who have put up with me playing an angry, smelly old man wearing nothing but a loincloth for several years. To my mother and stepfather for always being there for me, even if I'd prefer they not know what I write about in my spare time.

A heartfelt acknowledgement goes to my editor, Lottie Hayes-Clemens, whose invaluable insights and guidance shaped my work for the better in a thousand little ways. I am also indebted to the remarkably talented artists, Maxime Desmettre, for his captivating depiction of the cursed city of Elderstay, and Carson Lowmiller for his incredible vision of Gerome and Al, my unlucky protagonist and his resident demon. A special mention goes to my ARC readers who offered invaluable feedback and kind words during the finalisation of this project: my deepest thanks to Georgios Atsalis, Cheyenne Johnson, Hailey Renee Jones, Mackenzie Allquist, Amanda Vaughn, Miranda Griffith, Kathryn Vakavosaki, Sheree Parsons, Eefje Kamps, Ellen Connell, Krista Gordon, Kristie Wagner, John Clarke,

Rebecca Brigman-Holmes, Kate Haley, Catherine Bowser, Krystle Dullas, Shannon, Katrina Blidberg, Elena Piccioni, Ashley Rathborne, Emily Allain, Terra Hansing, Casey Barnes, Elizabeth Hellier, Erika Karr, Brody Hitchcock, Jasmine Sperring, Sara G. Cline, Shelby Tucker, Caitlin Guardino, Dallas Jarvis, Mic Villamayor, Chimene, Mrs Moa, Jenny Trevor, Quinn Mulvey, Becky Stokes, Sydney Pickens, Devi Letalis, Julia Cassell, Lehua Rivera, Erika Reffitt, Jeni King, Victoria Irwin, Teddi Edge, Ashley Niewiera, Tori Smithers, Ariana Leman, Dana Bailey, and Karyn Savage. You are all amazing.

And, finally, to the one with whom I share this pen name – my brother and partner in crime for being, well, excellent at drawing, having the best ideas, and being generally good at everything. I couldn't do this without you, Marco.

Content Warning

While intended to be fun and humorous, this book contains references to:

- *drug consumption*
- *violence using fantasy magic*
- *mass killings*
- *the death of a child*
- *suicidal thoughts*
- *demons*
- *demonic possession*
- *allusions to homophobia*
- *misogyny*
- *the occasional swear word*
- *a protagonist who is queer, ginger, and a gnome*
- *I reiterate: ginger.*

Readers who may be sensitive to these elements, please take note.

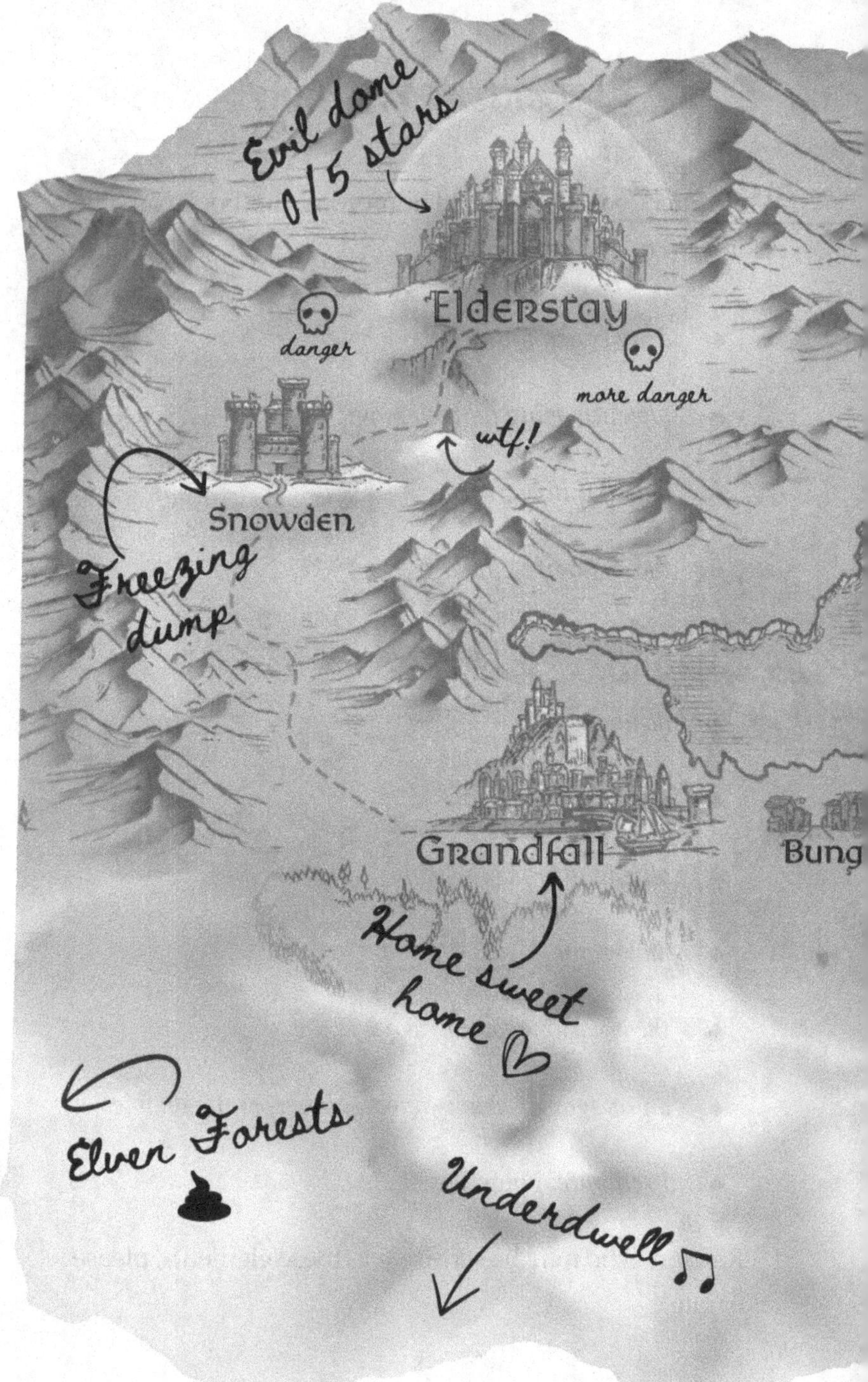

Evil dome
0/5 stars
Elderstay
danger
more danger
wtf!
Snowden
Freezing dump
Grandfall
Bung
Home sweet home
Elven Forests
Underdwell

TELLARIN

NORTHERN HEMISPHERE

Maracanda ⟶

Sultanate of
Sipera

PROLOGUE

To whom it may concern,

If you are reading this, I am indubitably dead. That's a good word to add a touch of whimsy to one's epitaph. *Here lies the indubitably dead so-and-so.* Please know, dear reader, I did not want to die. I very much liked living. As everyone could attest to at my local, the *Roaring Peacock*. Since you are looking at my disfigured and indubitably dead remains, let me tell you my name was Gerome.

Gerome the gnome.

Yes, I get that a lot.

This, dear reader, is my story as told by me. A version much unlike the one you may gather from campfire tales, read in books, or hear from your grandma in the years to come. If there are to be campfires, books, grandmas, or years to come, for that matter. This is the story of how I, Gerome, *magna cum laude* star pupil and, later, junior lecturer at the Arcane Polytechnic in Grandfall – a dashingly handsome and promising young man – doomed the world to the unspeakable horrors of the New Dark. I understand this will mean a big fat deal to you, as you contemplate the world's final days and all of existence being swallowed into the spiralling darkness of the Shade Planes. But, please, I must tell someone, anyone.

My bad. I am sorry.

As for why this happened, it began how all terrible things begin.

For a whiff of happiness.

And for want of hanky-panky.

Chapter One

THREE DAYS TO DOOMSDAY

It was only a few hours into the journey and I already wanted to go back to my suicidal life in Grandfall. My bum crack had been rubbed out by the cart's constant slipping and bouncing as we trundled along the mountain pass, and I was sure my travelling companion was going to kill me. Not intentionally, mind. Her bare hands and neck, the little skin she had exposed to the icy breeze, were covered in sand-coloured blotches and weeping crusts. Not to mention the eerie dust swirling about her person, billowing from beneath her sleeves in cloudy puffs of spores. I had scooted as far along as was polite before I attempted some small talk and amicably commented on a few ointments that may help her skin ailment. Aside from granting me a deathly look from under her hood, the young woman said nothing. One glance had been enough to determine she was not the kind of person with whom you swap idle chats.

While the cart driver and my toxic fellow traveller took in the scenery, I discreetly removed my winter gloves and reached into the depths of my coat for one of my "medicinal" pouches. I had three leather pouches of note. In layperson's terms, a red one, a black one, and a yellow one. The latter was my favourite. I snorted a few dabs of its contents so hastily even someone looking directly at me would have assumed I had repressed a sneeze. I am embarrassed at the art form to which I have elevated my drug abuse. I am the most proficient powder-snorter in all the lands. If only my mother could see me now…

As my reality transmuted into a distorted and polychromatic improvement on itself, my euphoric brain became vaguely aware of the fact that we'd been overtaken by two horsemen. Even in my addled state, I could tell they were my types: riding white steeds and clad in silver armour, inlaid with religious symbols of fealty to some lord, god, or other entity of importance. The two champions charged ahead along the rugged, frost-ridden path, glinting like shards of light in the darkness of my cruel, twisted existence.

"Fucking heroes," mumbled the cart driver under his breath.

I was too befuddled by how interesting my hands had become to scold the driver for his unfair comment towards the embodiment of my healthier sexual fantasies. Soon, I drifted off to sleep.

I woke to a tongue like sawdust and a cart full of goblins.

"Come on, up-up, little man! Up-up!"

My eyes blinked open to find a long, sloping nose pressed against mine. My senses filled with cavernous pores interspersed with pimples, on a face that shared its features and complexion with that of a sewer rat's. Retrospectively, the bright-bolt was a bit of an overreaction. I pointed my index at the creature and an instinctive sparkle of magic shot from the tip of my finger. Luckily, when startled, I'm a poor shot, otherwise the goblin would have been collecting its face off the town square. The whip of blue light erupted from my fingertip and volleyed past the creature's ear before pulverising a chimney and eradicating a family of finches.

"You must be the *magic* gnome," stuttered the goblin, its lopsided mouth breaking into a tentative smile.

I graciously allowed the comment to encompass a fourteen-year doctorate in the arcane and thousands of hours of methodical magical training. After all, I'd almost shot the unfortunate bastard's head off. I gathered my possessions, meaning I checked my three pouches were still in my pocket, before descending the cart. One cursory glance around the place was enough to determine something was unusual about Snowden.

The few details I remembered of the letter I'd received had made mention of a *collaboration* of sorts. Yet, I had never expected to see humans – by far the least inclusive of races – working with goblins. I had not anticipated anyone to be working with goblins, to be honest. Our destination, an ancient keep atop a snowy mountaintop, up close displayed amalgamations of architecture and technology. This was to say, the thick stone walls were reinforced with rickety wooden palisades and poor workmanship. Snowden's earthy tones of rock and timber had been vandalised by a riot of colourful finger paintings. Effigies of forest sprites and lesser deities, fashioned with sticks and rotting pelts, peered over the battlements. Glinting fires, kept alive by alchemical rather than natural means, were lit all over the plaza at the entrances of makeshift huts. Amid the crackling flames, animated goblins huddled together, their boisterous laughter filling the air as they roasted all manner of small animals on spits.

I noticed the young woman who'd accompanied me had already ventured to a dimly lit corner of the courtyard. She appeared to be scowling at the commotion of people moving about their business, her arms wrapped tightly around her chest out of more than cold, I could tell. What I couldn't determine was her race. She was a bit slight for a human. Much too beardless to be a dwarf.

Too ugly to be an elf. Too attractive to be an orc. Perhaps she was a half-breed, even if – and I knew this better than most – there were some *serious* anatomical hurdles to overcome. Before my brain could proceed down that particular rabbit hole, I was distracted by one of my favourite sounds. Our cart driver had been handed a jingling bag of coins from a goblin and was leading his draft horse to the stables. As I followed his movements, I spotted two white steeds tied to a pitching post nearby.

"Hello-hello, gnome! So, you have the letter, gnome?" piped a voice in my general vicinity.

Another goblin had appeared. A she-goblin this time. I could tell because she smelled slightly better. Also, she was wearing glasses and holding a piece of parchment, an ensemble that made the creature seem five times smarter than I knew her to be.

"Yes," I said, retrieving a soggy folded letter from my boot and presenting it to her.

The she-goblin held the letter up to the light, possibly to prove she could read – an impressive accomplishment for a member of her kind.

"Good, yes-yes. Can you confirm your name is *Gerome*?"

"Yes."

"Yes-yes. And you are a *gnome*, Gerome?"

"Last I checked."

There was a pause. Suddenly, the goblin spluttered with laughter. "You're Gerome the gnome?"

I stretched my lips into a practised smile. "I get that a lot."

"Fun-fun! And you're a wizard, Gerome the gnome?"

"Proficient in the arcane arts. Elemental manipulation is my speciality. I have a minor in evasive magic," I added with a touch of condescension.

Her weaselly eyes widened with excitement. "I read here that you can make fireballs?"

"Oh, yes." It had been a very effective pickup line of mine. One I prayed wouldn't be successful in this instance. "I can make fireballs."

"Good-good! Follow me! Lord Brent wants to meet you, yes. In the Grand Hall."

I cast my eye over my shoulder and spotted the hooded young woman following a stone's throw behind us. She, too, was accompanied by a goblin, but was keeping her distance from the motley creature. In principle, I didn't mind goblins. They were some of the few people with whom I could see eye-to-eye. When you stand a little over four feet from the ground, everyone looks down on you. Aside from goblins, that is. Everyone – even "littler" people – looks down on goblins.

The bespectacled she-goblin led me to an imposing set of doors and pushed them open with obvious effort. We entered a spacious and balmy hall filled with the scent of roasting pork and smoking wood. The snowflakes that speckled my coat instantly melted away and some sensation returned to the tip of my nose and a few of my other appendages. I barely had time to cast my eyes about the vast room when two towering men in armour turned their attention to me. I had some vague notion I'd seen them before but my memory had been unreliable of late. One of the men removed his helmet to reveal a thick mane of black hair and a perfect, dimpled smile.

Before I had the time to smarten myself up a bit, the handsome man strode up to me and clapped me on the shoulder with knee-bending force.

"Hail you, gnome of Underdwell!" he greeted me in a tone fashioned to be both amicable and assertive.

I lifted a cautious hand. "Hail you back, human. From somewhere."

Underdwell. It was a bigoted assumption to presume I was from the gnomish homeland, since gnomes nowadays resided in most places around Tellarin. It annoyed me that he was right. I was from Underdwell. The bad part.

"I am Emir Bijan Al-Malek, Crown Prince of the Kingdom of Sipera and champion pledged to the Goddess of All-goodness, Radia. I am honour-bound to serve His Lordship of Snowden, Lord Brent." He splayed a hand towards the other steel-clad beefcake who appeared to be contemplating me through the thin slits in his helmet's visor. "This is my brother, Emir Najib Al-Malek. Also a prince of the Kingdom of Sipera. Also a champion pledged to the Goddess of All-goodness, Radia. Also honour-bound to serve His Lordship of Snowden, Lord Brent."

"Nice to meet you, champions of Sipera," I stated politely, looking from Bijan to Najib. "I'm Gerome the gnome."

I waited for it. Neither of them took a crack at me. They'd probably vowed away their sense of humour.

"This is Sha-sha," continued Bijan, who'd seemingly taken it upon himself to introduce me to everyone in the hall. "She is an old friend of our father, Khosrow the Magnificent and Sultan of Sipera. As a kindly fate would have it, our paths have crossed again. She, too, has answered the call to Lord Brent's noble cause."

I glanced past Bijan's statuesque figure to an olive-skinned woman sitting at a nearby table. In truth, Sha-sha appeared to be coiled rather than seated on the chair, in a position I would have scarcely called comfortable. Her skin, upon more careful inspection, was a shade of green and it possessed a silky – almost reflective – quality to it. As for her hair, it was raven black and had that unmistakable cut-around-bowl style. She flicked her tongue at me. It was forked.

I heard the door creak open again and, heralded by a miasma of sickly spores, the hooded young woman entered the hall, accompanied by a frazzled male goblin who swiftly scuttled towards the she-goblin who'd escorted me inside. I watched as, after a clipped and strident exchange in their native tongue, the pair took off towards the far end of the room and vanished through a side door. The newcomer pulled down her hood, and I realised she was even younger than I'd originally assumed. A girl in her late teens, barely an adult. Before the friendly Bijan could approach her to make another round of introductions, a commanding voice demanded our attention.

"Ah, you are all here!"

A mountain of a man descended from the upper level. Bearded and well proportioned, he was wearing a breastplate and a long crimson cloak which, in my mind, suggested he could afford to be in charge. Both these items bore the insignia I'd spotted on the banners on my way through Snowden's courtyard. The emblem of the House of Agris, one of many aristocratic human families that squabbled among themselves for power and prestige and whatnot. An ornate bronze helmet between crossed swords. As for his age, I knew time to be less charitable to humans, who grew old more rapidly than most intelligent species on Tellarin. For the sake of politeness, a prudent habit among gnomes was to halve how old you assumed a human to be to get a ballpark estimate. To me, he looked to be a hundred, so I would have put money on the man being about fifty. A tad younger than me.

"I am Lord Brent of Snowden. I trust you have all received your letters and know about the stakes and rewards of this mission."

Bijan nodded with much enthusiasm, his chest thrust out like a prize rooster's. "My brother and I are honoured to answer Your Lordship's call. There is no greater privilege than to be of service."

The spore-plagued girl folded her arms and stared daggers at the champions. Sha-sha did not speak and remained still. Even her blinking was sluggish. As for me, I mumbled under my breath, "Of course. Service. What fun."

Lord Brent's piercing eyes dithered on me for a moment. "We are lucky to have a magic caster in our midst. Gerome was most eager to join."

"I was?" I tried to grasp at the foggy details of my summoning. Between the fragments of drug-fuelled confusion, I recalled someone approaching me at the *Roaring Peacock*. I had taken up residence at the inn's corner table by the grimiest window. I'd lost my job and my city apartment in rapid succession. Partridge, the innkeeper, hadn't had the heart to evict his most persistent customer. The next thing I knew, there was a letter with my name on it requesting my presence in Snowden. Spellcasters are always in high demand. Due to strict codes of conduct regarding the use of magic, any witch or wizard worth their salt would have refused to take part in some measly lord's quest. Not me. I would have sold my soul for a bowl of potato chips and an ounce of happiness. I had skimmed through the letter, my eyes lingering on the part that assured me that, once the job was done, "land, titles, and riches shall be yours".

"I am seeking people with certain talents," continued Lord Brent. "Talents that will be necessary to face the challenging task ahead, one to which I have devolved much effort and resources without success: the liberation of Elderstay."

"Elderstay?" I mused. "I've heard of the place before."

I had come across a mention of the city in a book about magically imbued weaponry. I could not recall the details but it had something to do with an enchanted hat.

"Elderstay was the prize jewel of my House, founded by my ancestor and folk hero, Agris of the Lighthelm. The citadel was lost under the rule of the late Lord Edmund, along with the fabled helmet that has been passed down in my family for generations," Lord Brent added with an unpleasant curl of his lips.

"What's so challenging about taking back some old city?" asked the girl, unable or unwilling to conceal the hostility in her tone. It was the first time I'd heard her speak. The girl's voice was coarse like sandpaper, as if her tongue struggled to form the words. I imagined it might be out of lack of practice since she struck me as the sullen, brooding type. The swirling spores landed around her, forming a thin coating of dust on the stone floor and falling softly on the dead-eyed hunting trophies mounted on the nearby wall. Before Lord Brent could reply, there was a mechanical whir.

"You are sick."

I did a double-take. The silent Najib had spoken. His voice, not unlike the girl's, was gritty and odd. But there was something else too. It had an artificial quality to it. I guessed it was the helmet.

"I can help."

Najib moved with unexpected speed. As his gauntleted hand stretched towards the girl, she jumped back, teeth bared like a hissing cat's.

"Do not touch me!" she snarled. "Never touch me!"

The spores shot from her open palm, right through the grooves in Najib's helmet. I watched in horror as millions of particles poured into his visor, in what I could only assume would be Najib's bloodcurdling demise.

No one appeared to be as concerned as I was. Shasha was making weird neck movements, like a swaying cobra hypnotized by the sound of a charmer's flute. Lord Brent was visibly annoyed. Not even Bijan moved in Najib's defence. Yet there was something about his expression that suggested sobriety. No – sadness.

"Are you quite done – what was your name?" asked a frustrated Lord Brent, his hands curling tight around his belt.

"Polly," retorted the girl, showing no sign of relenting.

Lord Brent paused in a way that suggested a sudden thought had crossed his mind. He soon dismissed whatever it had been. It must not have been important. "Stop it, this instant!"

"Why are you still standing, champion?" snarled Polly. The angry spore jets discharging from her hand were starting to thin.

Najib said nothing. He simply stood, grounded and solemn, concealed under a casing of metal and, now, a thick sheen of spores.

"Najib," began Bijan in a calm and even tone. "Polly does not want your assistance. Return to my side."

"Very well, brother."

I stared in fascination as Najib lumbered back to Bijan as if nothing had happened. Since her strike had been ineffective, Polly skulked to a dark corner and glowered at us from a distance. I guessed she wasn't accustomed to social niceties and being civil in general.

"So," I began, mindful of how long it'd been since my last joy snuff. "Why do you require our assistance to take back this city, Lord Brent?"

"Eleven winters ago," resumed Lord Brent, clearly grateful for my intervention, "a magical barrier rose around Elderstay, trapping the inhabitants inside. The few survivors speak of black tendrils and yellow lights in the sky. Of death and destruction beyond imaginable. For years, I have yearned to retake the city. Not too long ago, I learned of a way to breach the barrier: a hex designed to tamper with the barrier's energetic signature…"

I had the distinct impression the man was parroting words he'd been told with little understanding as to their meaning. I distractedly picked at my nails before I noticed, with a chill of unease, Sha-sha's unblinking eyes boring into me. I swallowed and turned away, in time to catch Lord Brent's grave voice saying, "We'd begun training some of our magically inclined townsfolk to use the hex. It was as if whoever or whatever conquered Elderstay knew this. A flurry of vicious attacks began, first on travellers on the road and farmers in the remote outskirts of our region, then on the settlements of our goblin neighbours. All have been granted safe haven within these walls, but it is only a matter of time before our foes decide to seize Snowden. This is why I have called upon your talents, to assemble a taskforce of people both willing and capable of infiltrating Elderstay and taking down the evil from within."

"And it shall be done, Your Lordship!" boomed Bijan, raising his fist.

"For the reward," hissed Sha-sha.

Polly turned her sulky glare to Lord Brent. "What kind of attacks?"

He paused. "The undead kind. Awakened cadavers ambushing unwary victims at all times of day. Walking corpses setting goblin camps alight. We believe it to be the work of demons."

"Wait," I felt the little colour left in my face drain away, "no one said anything about demons! Isn't that a job for the Enchanted Institution?"

Lord Brent's pleasant features became a mask of aggravation. "The Institution let me know in a missive that they'd send an independent assessor to *appraise* the situation. Since the evil appeared to be confined to a single city – one so very far from the rest of civilisation – they did not see it as a priority. No offence to the wizarding community, but they're a bunch of bureaucratic, mulish paper-pushers."

"None taken," I mumbled insincerely.

"Is that going to be a problem, Gerome?"

"It's just…" I wasn't sure how to end my sentence. Every eye turned to me in a way I did not like. They beheld me not merely as a coward – which would have been fine because it was true. But as if I was inept. The oldest child in the room. I was reminded of that time my mother had asked me to go buy a bag of onions and, by no fault of my own, I came home with a pocketful of sweets and a pet hedgehog. I opted to take a break and deal with the loss of face later on. "No, of course not! Demons – pfft – no problem, easy-peasy. If you could excuse me for a moment…"

I strode past the champions, gave Polly and Sha-sha ample space, and pushed open a crack in the door wide enough to slip through.

Out in the freezing air, I stared at the gloomy sky overhead and the ragged flags billowing on their masts in the blustering wind, feeling my breaths come short. It was decided. I was going to leave this instant. I was going to march back to the cart and convince the driver to take me back to Grandfall.

Then it happened. A whisper. It always started with a whisper. And it was the reason I could not go home. The reason I had to stay. My hand fumbled inside my coat's inner pocket.

Not now.

Gerome...

Not now, Al.

What is the matter, Gerome?

You're what's the matter. You're always what's the matter!

Come now, little friend, do you not want to play a game?

No! No games! Go away!

My shaking fingers found the dark pouch I'd been looking for. What remained of my once comfortable affluence – aside from my tattered clothes beneath the coat I'd borrowed off Partridge's eleven-year-old, and the holey boots on my feet – amounted to three leather pouches concealed on my person. Each contained different and indistinguishable powders that went by the street names of *yaydust*, *roard*, and *sleeper*. The way I told them apart was yellow for joy, red for courage, and black for relaxation. Admittedly, a few copious snorts later, I knew I had taken relaxing too far.

I can only imagine the impression I must have cast on my new patron, as I re-entered the hall grinning like a madman, my pupils dilated to the size of dinner plates. Lord Brent kept directing worried glances my way throughout the rest of the meeting. I'm unsure how many bursts of uncontrollable laughter made it out of my mouth in the misty line between fiction and reality. I registered nothing of the subsequent conversation, except that we were given a small advance on payment to stock up on rations and gear for the journey ahead.

"You have one hour," stated Lord Brent, his words reaching me distorted and warped through my medicinal influences. "There is an apothecary in Snowden where you may replenish your supplies. When you are done, I expect to see you at the campsite west of Snowden's outer walls. After that, you'll be on your way to Elderstay."

As my future companions walked out of the Grand Hall, except Sha-sha, who sort of glided, Polly slunk up beside me.

"I can get you something better," she murmured, stooping down level with my ear. Her hoarse, unused voice made me feel uneasy.

"Not sure what you're talking about," I countered, keen to evade the topic and the plume of toxic spores that lingered in her vicinity.

"It's far better than the stuff you've been taking, gnome."

My eyes darted about to confirm we weren't being overheard. "What *stuff*?"

Polly opened her palm to reveal a single orange mushroom, no larger than a marble.

"Take this. Something tells me you'll like it."

Without further ado, I popped the mushroom straight into my mouth: a testament to how little I valued my own life of late.

Polly wasn't a liar. That unassuming fungus made it all instantly disappear. My worries about demons. My worries about Elderstay. My worries in general. My ability to worry. Yet, unlike the effects of my usual drugs, I remained clear-headed, my brain uncluttered from hallucinations and obsessive thoughts. For the first time in about a year, I felt like myself. It was a high I never wanted to come down from. In this mental state, I could deal with anything. Even *Al*.

I handed her the bag of coins Lord Brent had given me, without as much as counting the contents.

"More, please."

Chapter Two

WALKING NIGHTMARES

"Now, let us go over this one more time, Najib. The lovely Mrs Tilda at *Raving Remedies* told us that the silvery concoction with the cork top will make you feel rested. The ointment in the bone-shaped jar seals wounds. These herbs in the woven flax container will facilitate rapid digestion and prevent constipation…"

I rolled my eyes in exasperation. We were trudging together through Snowden's winter wonderland, at varying levels of aptitude. Polly was pelting ahead like a woodland creature, followed a short distance behind by Sha-sha whose pursuit felt mildly predatorial. I, on the other hand, would occasionally vanish waist-deep in the snow before being retrieved by a swing of Najib's huge metal arm. The two brothers marched on either side of me, matching my pace in what I could only assume was a thoughtful show of comradery. Bijan was peering into his satchel, holding out a vial or parcel in turn, and describing to Najib the alleged effects of each of their recent purchases. The ones they had so responsibly bought with Lord Brent's money. As I reached into my pocket to probe the handful of spongy mushrooms I'd acquired from Polly, I wondered if I'd been half as smart.

"… and should be taken with a pinch of charcoal and a glass of water, limited to a spoonful a day to improve your ability to see in the dark."

Bijan's thoroughness might have been an endearing show of brotherly love, had it not been the fifth time he had gone over the remedies' effects since we'd left the keep. I could only conclude that Najib suffered from short-term memory loss or was not the smartest finger in the glove. By the time we got to the campsite, I was wet up to my crotch and in a foul mood, and prepared to force-feed Bijan his stupid vials.

"There you all are," bellowed Lord Brent, his lips parting into a relieved grin. He approached us, flanked by a pair of pike-holding guards – the standard accessories of every proper lord. His broad, hirsute face arranged itself into a friendly expression. Yet, from the way his feet veered every few moments in the direction of Snowden's keep, I knew he was as keen for us to be on our way as I was to be done with this mission. "The recruits are gathered and ready to follow your lead."

We silently followed the Lord and his escort as they led us through the campsite. My eyes were swift to gather disheartening details. Rickety tents had been pitched in a semicircle around what I supposed was an attempt at a training course. A few straw dummies stood in the middle of the course, propped up against wonky poles and splayed at odd angles. I spotted a practice range outside the boundaries of the encampment, the general intactness of the target boards suggesting they were seldom used, or the archers were exceptionally lousy marksmen.

At the sight of us, the campsite's occupants – forty or fifty strong, at least – hurried to form a series of disorganised lineups. I cast my gaze upon the assorted militia – humans and goblins of varying ages – that were to accompany us on our journey to Elderstay. The only commonality was the shabbiness of their equipment and their worrisome frowns. Some wore flimsy recurve bows with fraying strings over their shoulders, others carried blunt, rusted swords strapped to their waists. Much to my amazement, I noticed several figures holding wooden staffs in their midst. I hoped they were the ones used to channel arcane potential and not the assisted-walking kind. Most of the spellcasters sported grey hair and fake teeth. That didn't surprise me. Magic was an old person's game. Not *this* old, though.

"Listen up, good people of Snowden!" Lord Brent called out over the murmurings of the crowd. "And of surrounding areas and cave systems!" he added as the goblins began muttering their objections. "Today, we stand not as humans or goblins, but as a united force, bound by a shared purpose. You have volunteered to be part of something greater than yourselves. A noble quest to avenge our dead and claim our future. Soon we are to take back Elderstay and purge the evil that has tainted our lands. This journey will not be without peril, but do not fear. Your commanders are people of talent who will see to it that you are returned whole and healthy to your families! With capable men and women leading the charge, and the gods on our side, we cannot fail. Are you ready to serve your home, your country, and your Lord?"

There was a short-lived and unenthusiastic clamour from the crowd.

"And you will all be rewarded handsomely upon your return."

This afforded the Lord a far heartier cheer.

"If we return at all," I griped under my breath. I could not quell the burning unease the man's speech had ignited within me. These people were not fighters. And I could barely look after myself, let alone ensure others stayed "whole and healthy".

I caught Bijan's eye. There was a vein pulsing beneath his chiselled jawline.

"Are you willing to give your lives for the liberation of Elderstay?" he asked. Bijan's voice soared effortlessly over the stunned silence that followed. His question, unlike Lord Brent's, was not rhetorical.

There were several meek cries of assent, yet Bijan did not seem satisfied. Like a petulant eagle, he marched amid the troops and scoured the faces in the rabble one by one, until he found what he was looking for.

"You three," he called, pointing at a handful of teenagers who were standing close together. "What are your names?"

"Us?" asked a boy, gesturing at himself before nudging his tight-lipped companions. "I'm Mike. He's Charles. This one's my sister, Dana."

"Are you willing to die?"

"Preferably not, sir. Yeah, it's dangerous. But Lord Brent said we're just meant to open the barrier. He says it's your lot that are gonna go inside, not us." The boy eyed Brent's stony expression and dropped his gaze, hands shaking.

It was dawning on me that I must have missed certain important details from the briefing while skipping up my powder-sprinkled staircase to bliss.

I watched as Najib took his brother's side and boomed from beneath his cumbersome helmet, "Do not come."

Lord Brent looked from one armoured champion to the other, as if they'd gone insane. "What did you say to them, Emir Najib?"

"My brother is right," said Bijan, his tanned features and gemstone eyes gleaming in the pale sunlight. "There is nothing worse than fear. I want those under my command to desire our glorious quest with all their hearts, not to be tempted merely by the lure of gold or the threat of retribution. There will be other times to test your-selves. Go home. You are free from your oath."

I spotted Polly stick a finger in her throat as if induc-ing herself to vomit. Sha-sha grimaced in displeasure.

"Nah, Your Sirship," muttered the one called Charles. "We can't. We need the cash. We gotta go to Elderstay."

"Upon my return, I will give you three the money you were promised," Bijan stated firmly. "Or so Radia smite me."

"No!" spat an exasperated Lord Brent. He was glar-ing at the three teenagers, red in the face. "If you renege on your word and take one step out of this campsite, you will be branded cowards and not see a single coin!"

Bijan lifted a hand. "Lord Brent, I ask that you allow the youngsters' payment to come out of my reward."

"Are you saying we can go home, sir? And still get paid?" asked Dana. She was catching on.

I watched with moderate interest as a sparkle of understanding rippled through the troops. Bijan may have inadvertently killed our budding venture before we'd moved an inch towards Elderstay. Telling people they're still going to get compensated without risking life and limb is no way to run an army. Yet, I couldn't help but feel the faintest pinch of admiration for Emir Bijan, a man who so ardently believed in innocent no-tions such as integrity and justice. It must be nice, not to have been shanked in the nether regions by life.

To my astonishment, and probably Lord Brent's, only the three teens left the campsite. I guessed the others were too uncomfortable with the idea of going back on their word. Perhaps they thought Bijan could not afford to pay them all out. Or maybe it was Bijan. He had that effect on people. His decency was contagious.

The archers and the soldiers, comprising the more youthful-looking goblins and humans, were divided into two groups, one led by Najib and one by Bijan. Polly was not trusted to command anything more than a small group of scrawnier goblins who were meant to be carrying our tents. As for Sha-sha and I, we were given nominal leadership over a handful of elderly staff holders, all of whom were exclusively human. Goblins were among the few races incapable of mastering the arcane.

"I trust you won't give any away," Lord Brent growled in a low voice, taking Sha-sha and me aside. "It took us months to find people with sufficient magical skill to master the hex that will take down the barrier. You cannot succeed without them!"

If my recruitment process was anything to go by, I guessed Lord Brent had sought among his subjects anyone with the slightest spell-casting inclination, perceived or otherwise. But cantrips for preserving fish and uncurdling milk were a tad different from blowing up a demon's energy barrier. Also, it looked like Brent had kidnapped them all from a rest home.

"No. We will keep them. *Keep them all.*" Sha-sha's tone was unnecessarily creepy.

Lord Brent eyed the green woman as she stared insistently at her regiment, before shifting his gaze to me. "You know how to lead, gnome? Get respected?"

"I used to be a lecturer at the Arcane Polytechnic in Grandfall." The mushroom was doing wonders for my confidence. "I think I can handle a handful of apprentices. Even *veteran* ones such as these."

To prove a point, I allowed a wisp of flame to dance along my knuckles until I almost burned myself.

Lord Brent appeared satisfied. With one last nod, he wished us well and left.

Not a half-hour later, we were packed and ready to go. I looked about as the tents were lifted and the gear heaved, to Bijan and Najib who gave our mission some semblance of professionalism, at Polly bossing around her regiment like they were her minions, and Sha-sha interspersing moments of great stillness with spurts of excited movement as she slid about the busy campsite. As for me, I allowed myself to think this would be easy money. That we'd be in and out of Elderstay in a day. By this time next month, I'd be halfway to Maracanda, where my heart-wrenchingly expensive treatment was rumoured to be.

My optimism was sorely misplaced.

The first leg of the trip was a breeze. Up until the moment we found blood spattered across the snow.

"It's fresh," said Sha-sha, her forked tongue flashing briefly between her thin lips.

Polly kneeled and ran a fistful of reddened mush through her fingers. "Could be an animal…" she muttered, in a way that suggested she doubted it.

"We should investigate," stated Najib, in his odd drone.

Bijan agreed. "I will tell our troops to stop. We'll move forward and see what we find."

I watched as the four of them followed the crimson trail that drew a grim path through the white landscape, straight into the low-hanging mist ahead. I was feeling a little nauseous. Had it not been for the expectant eyes of my regiment and an uneasy tingling in the pit of my stomach, I would have happily stayed behind pretending to cast some fact-finding spells. Against my better judgement, my feet began an unenthusiastic trudge after my companions.

"Something is wrong," said Sha-sha. "No footsteps. No drag marks. No scents of beasts. Only spilled blood."

"Maybe it snowed," mused Najib, ever the thinker.

"No!" snapped Polly. "Snow would have covered the blood as well. This is so weird."

"Then, whoever was bleeding this badly must have been levitating off the ground," I offered. It was a joke. But the way my associates stared at me gave my words a chilling credibility.

The grisly trail continued for more or less fifty yards, traced in more fluids than any one human body might contain. That's when we found the victim. A middle-aged woman, mangled beyond recognition. Her body was splayed, face up and limbs apart, inside what appeared to be a ritual circle. Unintelligible glyphs marked the perimeter, drawn in – my favourite – more blood.

"Wow.' Polly stopped at the edge of the circle and leaned forward. "Looks like she was ripped open by something."

"The corpse's organs have been torn out,' Sha-sha's eyes narrowed at the gruesome scene. "The liver is missing."

"What a ghastly and fiendish sight," declared Bijan, his hand on the hilt of his greatsword. "No doubt some kind of nefarious sorcery was being attempted here! What do you think, Gerome?"

I had some choice words I would have liked to contribute to this conversation. Pity no one heard them over the sound of me throwing up.

"I will examine," mumbled Najib in his hollow voice.

"No!" I managed, wiping my chin. "Don't step inside! At least, let me do a *thing* first."

I repressed the impulse to swallow another mushroom or snort a line of powder. I needed steely concentration and clear taste buds if this was to work. I took a cleansing mouthful of fresh snow and flexed my fingers.

One of the first spells an apprentice wizard is taught at any decent arcane establishment is how to detect magic itself. Every spellcaster leaves a unique magical imprint. A calling card of sorts. The brain translates these hidden traces via the tip of the tongue. Wizards who've been dabbling in forbidden sorcery taste like lemon sherbet. Evil witches like blue cheese. Inexperienced spellcasters are chewy and sweet, like gummy bears.

I made a couple of complicated gestures, mostly for show, and focused on my mouth. As I suspected. The worst possible flavour: strawberries.

"It's a trap," I warned. "This is the work of a demon. If you go through, there's no knowing what might happen."

"I will go." Before I could do more than swear in gnomish, Najib stepped through the blood circle.

I knew instantly something bad had happened. My first clue came when Najib's body twisted backwards at a funny angle, and his legs began to stagger towards the black pillar. *Wait, how did I miss that?* A towering pillar, its surface like smooth obsidian, rose ominously in the middle of the blood circle. It's crazy the things you fail to notice when there is a disembowelled body hogging all the attention.

"Brother!" screamed Bijan. "Come back!"

I clasped a hand around Bijan's belt, the least complicated reaching point for a gnome. "Don't, or the same thing will happen to you!"

Unexpectedly, Polly took a step inside the circle. I watched in horror as she froze, rooted to the spot, before she began thrashing about with tell-tale signs of demonic possession. She, too, started moving towards the pillar in jittery, erratic strides.

"For Radia!" Bijan had decided to join in the idiocy. Invoking his deity, he charged into the fray his sword high above his head – and he too, inevitably, succumbed to the wicked thrall and began a wobbly pilgrimage towards the black pillar.

Sha-sha and I swapped an uneasy glance from the safe space outside the blood circle.

"You next," she hissed.

"Ladies first," I countered.

Najib was the first to make it to the pillar. I watched as the metal-headed simpleton drew a knife from the girdle strapped around his waist and ran it across his gauntleted hand. The blade tore through the soft leather on the palm as if it were made of butter, evidence of Najib's considerable strength as much as the quality of his weaponry. But I did not see him bleed. Not a single drop. He tried again. And again. Still nothing. I stared in morbid fascination as the man stabbed deeper and deeper into his own flesh. The knife returned dry every time.

"Let me!" snarled Polly, staggering up from behind him. She pulled a serrated dagger from her belt and slashed it carelessly across her wrist. Blood gushed from her wound and dripped in rivulets down her arm, staining the snow a deep scarlet.

Polly pressed her bleeding gash on the dark surface.

At that exact moment, the obsidian pillar screeched. Or, whatever was inside the pillar did. A spine-chilling scream that couldn't possibly belong to anything birthed by a benevolent god. The pillar began to glow with a ghoulish yellow light. Like charred skin from flesh, something crackled and peeled off the pillar's smooth exterior. It's hard to describe what exactly we were looking at. It resembled a shadow. The shadow of something with mangled hair, strewn about a featureless face, and a torn, gaping mouth from which came another abyssal screech. One so endless it felt like it might have begun in the cradle of darkness itself. The shadow soared into the air and revolved around the blood circle's three interlopers, clawing at them with hands like thorny branches.

My companions blinked and looked about, finally coming to their senses.

"What happened?" I heard Bijan say.

"Get out of there, you stupid—"

They never got to hear the ever-so-apt epithets I had devised. Something grabbed my ankle from beneath the snow. I fell face first in the cold, white powder, and turned to see what had seized me.

A skeleton hand.

In a split second, I spotted another. And another. And one more. You get the idea. Bodies in various stages of decay had begun sprouting from the snow in a terrifying rendition of a spring bloom.

"Oh, bollocks."

A bolt of energy shot from my index finger and blew the bony hand off at the wrist. I got up to realise I was surrounded. The walking cadavers were inching closer, their arms swinging aimlessly about in an attempt to grab me. Their depth perception must have been shocking.

Sha-sha was nowhere to be seen.

I caught the unmistakable sounds of battle and glanced in the direction of the black pillar. Most of my other companions were locked in close-range combat with the shrieking shadow. I had to admit Bijan looked majestic as he whirled his greatsword through the air with both hands. While beautiful to behold, his attacks were useless. The shadow had a smoky consistency, impervious to even the best-delivered blade strokes. Polly was not quite as glorious but was yielding better results. The sandy dust that oozed from her person had formed a defensive sphere around her. Every time the shadow came within reach, the spores would coagulate into vinelike whips and fend off any attempts to approach her. It was magic. Just not the mainstream kind. That's what happens when those with magical inclinations receive no formal training.

Najib, who'd clearly not caught up with the situation, was still pounding his hand against the pillar. A crack had begun to appear. Still no sign of Sha-sha, that *snake*—

That's when I got punched in the face. Flat on my back, my nose gushing and my teeth feeling loose, I heard my inner tormentor chuckle.

Care for some help, little man?

I'd rather fondle a gorilla with debatable hygiene.

Suit yourself.

Whatever mental retort I had lined up was stifled by the fleshless fingers wrapped around my windpipe. One of the skeletons had grabbed me. All I could make out, through my throbbing eardrums, was the terrifying silence of the dead and the eerie grinding of bones kept together by strings of rotting tendons and pure evil. With my last ounce of strength, another ray of light shot from my finger. My attacker's skull exploded, showering my face in bone fragments.

Dragging myself to my feet, I cussed under my breath. I couldn't do this for much longer. Beads of sweat were pouring off of me. Accurate magic – the kind that reliably limits its destructiveness to the intended target – requires tremendous concentration. *Inaccurate* magic on the other hand…

Fireball.

I'd rather not. Too lethal.

Well, it's not like you can make these animated corpses any more dead.

Maybe you have a point, Al.

I always have a point, Gerome.

A fiery bead began spinning at exponential speed in my palm, emitting the heat of a miniature sun. Holding my wrist steady with my other hand, I aimed at the closest skeleton.

Do it. Destroy them all.

I hesitated, a nagging feeling in my gut. Polly and Bijan were a mere thirty feet away. Najib was positioned just a little further. Once cast, there was no stopping a fireball. If I missed the skeleton, I had no real certainty as to the direction the fireball may choose to take on its way back to the target. Not to mention the hellish ground-shattering blast…

I let my hand drop to my side. The incandescent blob of annihilation sizzled out and died with its caster's wavering resolve.

You're pathetic.

As another staggering corpse approached me, its fleshless fingers outstretched and grasping, I opted to put my academic minor to good use instead. Practitioners of the arcane arts look down on evasive magic. It's considered *slippery*. It is not as glamorous as conjuring a phoenix or shooting fiery beams from your hands. Yet, while evasive magic couldn't score you a date, it could definitely bail you out of one.

It took most wizards a decade to master invisibility. I'd managed it in two years. Then, I proceeded to go beyond it. I had mastered evasion to a level that far surpassed that of my former teachers. I could make myself so invisible, I wasn't even here anymore. As if I'd winked out of existence altogether. I'd found pockets in the universal ridges in which I could fold my being away and hide until it was safe to come out. I had made my very own ten-by-ten bachelor pad in no-space. I'm shamelessly proud of that one.

Back to my skeleton.

It went to gauge my eyes out. Or it would have, had I still been there. Unbeknown to it, I had become invisible and was running towards the treeline, as fast as my short-but-proportionate legs would carry me.

I needn't have bothered. Suddenly, a gigantic tail slid across the snow, lifting a tsunami of ice and levelling everything in its path. It collided with the skeletons at waist height. Their twig-like bodies lost integrity and were catapulted into the sky, femurs and ribs raining down on me. I could do little more than watch with mounting anxiety, as an enormous serpent emerged from the white landscape. Things couldn't get any worse. Until I realised the shock of witnessing the slimy beast burst out of nowhere had returned me to the realm of the visible.

"This has not been my day," I groaned.

I readied a fireball. For real this time.

The huge V-shaped pupils glared at me in a way both familiar and unsettling.

"Sha-sha?" I asked, letting my hand drop an inch.

The creature blinked.

"Sha-sha," I continued, struggling with the notion. "Are you a *snake*?"

I mean, why was I surprised? It's not like there hadn't been clues. Her unusual skin tone. The forked tongue. That terrible haircut.

The snake whipped its head into the air. With much bending and coiling, which I'd rather forget so close to dinnertime, Sha-sha resumed the shape of a naked, greenish woman with an unfashionable hairdo. As she went about retrieving her robes and pointedly ignoring my nauseated expression, I turned to see how the others were faring.

There was a thunderous boom.

I gawked, transfixed, as long fractures climbed the obsidian pillar, and black ichor began oozing from the cracks. The shadow gave one final ear-piercing shriek and, with a flash of pure darkness, it vanished. The pillar shattered into a million fragments. Glass-like shards rained down on us, turning to dust before they could cut skin. The unleashed demonic arcana whipped back my hair and rippled through the wintry air. The shadow's scream reverberated in my chest for some time after that. I knew it carried a haunting promise.

This was only the beginning.

Chapter Three

HIDDEN ENEMY

As we had a chance to ascertain a few moments later, the disappearance of the screeching monstrosity appeared to be thanks to Najib. While Polly and Bijan had been distracting the blasted creature, Najib had been pounding his fist against the pillar until it cracked. Correlation does not imply causation, but it seemed like a big coincidence that once the pillar was destroyed, the noisy shadow had returned to whatever dismal place it had slithered out from.

I was allowed a short moment of reprieve to count my teeth before Bijan asked me – in no uncertain terms – to walk back to our squadrons and tell them it was safe to come over.

"And no need to alarm our people. Just inform them the evil is vanquished and they have nothing to fear. We will get them safely to Elderstay. I, Emir Bijan Al-Malek, swear upon Radia that I will lay down my life for any one of them. As I'm sure any of you would," he added, pulling off his helmet and running a powerful hand through his curly wet hair.

As I trudged back towards the recruits, I decided to omit that last part in virtue of it being patently *garbage*. I was unsure when Bijan had become the de facto leader of our small and dysfunctional group, but I found it hard to question him and his sculpted buttocks.

When I returned with our regiments in tow, I spotted Bijan standing close to Najib, a deep frown line creasing his forehead.

Something pricked at my heart as I saw Bijan's face darken. I was the seventh of thirteen brothers. *Lucky seven*, according to my mother. Even though, at times, I had wanted to thin out my siblings' numbers with my own bare hands, I knew that expression. Najib's armoured glove was warped and twisted at a funny angle. I could only imagine what his hand looked like within it.

"I am well," confirmed Najib, in his dull drone. If he was in pain, it was impossible to tell.

Bijan didn't speak, but his eyes were fixed on his brother's gnarled limb.

"Take your gauntlet off, Najib," I said, approaching them both in what I believed to be a helpful tone. "I am no doctor, but the swelling—"

Bijan cut me short. "There is no time. We must keep going."

I opened my mouth, but seeing Bijan's grim scowl I closed it again. Seemed like an unsound and unhealthy proposition to me, but I didn't dare challenge the champion. Neither did Polly and Sha-sha. Mostly because they didn't care.

Bijan drove us hard from that moment onwards. We travelled for three hours without pause through the barren and frozen wasteland, before we met our next hurdle. A colossal wall of ice, lodged between two mountain peaks, barred our way. The sheer size of the massive frosty formation made my neck hurt and my eyes pinch. There were talks about going back to Snowden and waiting till spring, but the goblins in our group were quick to spot an entrance. A gaping fissure that sliced a path through the impregnable barrier. Upon closer inspection, the passage was wide enough for two carts moving in tandem, and as deep and dark as a politician's closet. To me, it screamed, "TRAP!"

"Are you sure this is the only way to Elderstay?" I asked, approaching the goblins who'd found the opening. The loud gathering that was packed together chittering in their native tongue – a collection of sharp snorts and guttural noises – stopped abruptly. They turned to me with reverent curtsies. I supposed the news had gotten around about the gnome that could summon fireballs. "Surely, we can bypass this huge ice cube?"

"No-no, can't," grumbled an older goblin with braided silver hair and a nose so prominent it shadowed his feet.

"Too cold, too snowy. In winter this is the only way, yes-yes."

"Bingop-ul's right, he is," seconded a she-goblin with wonky teeth and thick black eyebrows. "He's a *permgre* – he's seen many seasons and knows these parts best."

Years ago, I had taken a summer school paper entitled, *Goblins: Intellectually Stunted or Just Bluffing,* which was turning out to be remarkably handy. The word *permgre* meant "honoured elder". Which denoted any goblin that made it past the age of thirty, without dying of dysentery or in a knife fight.

As if to appease my sceptical expression, the she-goblin added with a gleeful nod, "The path between the mountains is a lot nicer in summer, yes-yes."

"Then, it's decided," stated Bijan, before the rest of us could object. "Into the icy jaws we go."

There was some hesitation among us all, but soon our regiments had formed a semi-orderly column and began the journey through the cleft in the ice. We walked in silence, jumping at the slightest creaking in the glacial mass and the subtlest breath of wind until the boredom of the slow journey made us complacent. I found myself sidling up to Polly who happened to be falling behind. That was where I fell all the time.

"Want to show me that cut?" I asked, trying not to inhale the thick mist that hung around the girl.

"No." Polly drew her poorly bandaged wrist to her chest. "Don't touch me."

I could have easily left it at that, but being an extrovert is a curse. "You fought well back there, Polly. Your spellcasting was crude but effective. I was a lecturer at the Arcane Polytechnic in Grandfall. I recognise talent when I see it."

She grinned. The first time I'd seen her lips curl upwards. She seemed almost approachable. "You're a prick, gnome."

I took it in my stride. When you're the shortest guy in most rooms, you develop thick skin and selective hearing. "Well, you're not one of my students. But, if you were, I'd say your powers are impressive."

"I bet you're the only one who thinks that."

"I'm sure the others do too."

"No, they don't. They're not like you."

Before she could tell me what she'd meant by that, there was a scream.

"Everyone, look up! Look, yes-yes!" yelled a terrified goblin amid our group.

I did. A gaunt figure was standing on the edge of the crevasse, glaring down at us. As I scoured the margins of the chasm against the pale skyline, I spotted dozens of them. Maybe hundreds. Maybe more. Their sunken faces turned in our direction with putrid arms clasped at their sides, leaning forward in a macabre bow.

I didn't need a degree in military manoeuvres to know that being at the bottom of an ice crevice is what any decent strategist would call a *balls-up.*

The sound of metal and string rang through the passageway as swords were drawn and arrows cocked. In their panic to react, the recruits nipped each other with the edges of their weapons. We were squashed like sardines in a tin can, and – alas – I could taste strawberries.

The corpses merely stared, with eyeless sockets and lipless mouths. Cadavers in a more recent state of decay than the ones we'd faced hours earlier.

"They're trying to scare us!" roared Bijan, ever brimming with confidence. "But we have the All-good Radia on our side and courage in our hearts!"

It was hard to topple such conviction but, ten minutes of nervous immobility later, I ventured a whisper. "They haven't made a move. Perhaps we should carry on walking."

"Gerome is right," snapped Polly, her raspy voice rising to a shout. "I want my reward. And we're not getting any closer to Elderstay stuck here in this freezing hole!"

"It'll be dark soon," Sha-sha hissed in agreement.

Bijan glanced at us, then at his silent brother. "What do you think, Najib?"

"I am well," replied the armoured man, contemplating the ground with great interest, or as much of it as he could make out through the thin slits in his helmet.

"Then I must bend to the will of my companions." Bijan's expression was grim as he whipped his head back towards the recruits. "We will continue, but keep your weapons drawn and ready. If the foul enemies attack, we shall send them back to the black void from whence they came!"

I thought "whence" was a bit over the top, but everyone did as they were told.

I'm not sure when along the journey the dark murmurings began. After all, I have a zero-tolerance policy when it comes to voices in my head. But the closer we got to Elderstay, the louder the whispers became. Quickly downing one of Polly's mushrooms and snorting a pinch of powder, in case the fungi weren't enough, the world around me dissolved. The ominous rumblings were lost like drops in the ocean. The rest of the journey through the icy passage was peaceful for me. A gentle trudge through the snow. One in which I paid far too much attention to how cool it was that my footprints fit my boots, rather than my companions' worries and moods. Had I been more observant, I might have noticed this was the moment it all started to go wrong.

I was just too high.

Stopping for the night became the obvious choice as we emerged from the ice wall's narrow channel into a barren, rocky expanse, blanketed in a thin layer of frost. The sun was winking away behind the mountains, and we'd begun losing sight of each other in the fading light.

Bijan would have kept going, had it not been for the reassurances of the local goblins that we'd be in Elderstay by midday if we left at dawn. The over-keen champion finally agreed to make camp and rest here for the night.

Five large marquees were pitched with the expectation that each of us would sleep with our allotted squadrons. I had other plans. But I did help kindle the fires – far easier than gathering wood and pitching tents but fetched way more *wows*. After hanging our boots to dry and feasting on desiccated meat and a tin of peas, we all started to relax. Mostly thanks to the goblins. The honoured elder Bingop-ul and a handful of his kinfolk retrieved a keg of foul-smelling grog they'd smuggled with them, unbeknown to Lord Brent. They claimed it was a cultural right or something. As it turned out, alcohol loosened the humans up and made goblins unexpectedly gifted singers.

We had a bit of a bash that night. At least, some of us did. Sha-sha had forbidden everyone from having any fun. Polly had gone to bed in one of the marquees, so many of her goblin recruits had joined mine. I suspected it was because no one was keen to join her in the tent so soon, toxic mist and all. Bijan dropped in to inform us of how mind-altering substances were a scourge on society. With the paragon of buzzkills hovering about, the fighters and archers under his and Najib's command begrudgingly retired for the night, leaving my elderly spellcasters and the goblins to party.

As the night progressed and the cold set in, there were talks of moving our merriment to one of the marquees. That was my cue. Despite the balding human with a silver moustache – which summed up the appearance of many members of my squadron – who had been giving me flirtatious glances all night, I got up to find a solitary place to sleep. I hadn't been able to indulge my carnal desires as much as I'd have liked since Al had sunk his nasty, evil claws in my mind. My demonic ailment was always worse when I was drowsy or distracted. I could not afford to let my guard down.

"Goodnight, everyone!" I called over the protestations of the merry gathering. "Drink up! Have fun! Don't do anything I wouldn't do!"

Well, that narrowed it down. On my way out, I skipped over loose shoes and ducked under airing cloaks and trousers, through a maze of scents and snores. A handful of Bijan's soldiers were on patrol. For sensible reasons, such as ensuring we wouldn't get our drunken asses butchered in our sleep by dead people.

I spotted a boulder outside the campsite. Perfect. I could sneak behind it and smuggle off into my personal patch of no-space where no one would bother me—

I hadn't expected to see a mirror. It was leaning against the boulder, gleaming in the moonlight. It was as tall as a grown human, well crafted yet unpretentious, with speckled discolourations around the edges. There was a small crack in the top right-hand corner where a piece had been chipped off. I caught a glimpse of myself in it. I looked twice my age. My face was marked by worry lines and sleep deprivation. Add a dollop of drug abuse and a failing liver, and the result was a sallow complexion that jarred with my vivid red hair. I was just fifty-five. I'd barely hit manhood. I'd barely *enjoyed* manhood.

"Gerome? What are you doing?"

"Bijan!" I stammered, turning on the spot. "I didn't see you there!"

I hadn't immediately recognised him. Without his silver armour and full-face helmet, his black locks hung loosely around his face, framing his cheekbones and falling alluringly over his vibrant aquamarine eyes. He had changed into an elaborate silk shirt and baggy trousers which tightened at the waist and ankles. Even in casual wear, Bijan was effortlessly dashing. Unlike yours truly.

"That's mine," he explained. "It was too large for my tent."

So, I wasn't the only one who'd scorned the crowded marquees. I followed his gaze to an unassuming tent, pitched on the boundary of the campsite. I had thought the handsome crown prince of Sipera as humble as his tents. But lugging around a full-size mirror on a quest to kill a demon suggested otherwise.

I absentmindedly ran a hand through my overgrown fringe. "Why bring such a huge mirror on a mission?"

Bijan hesitated before replying. "Mirrors are the sacred instruments of Radia. She is the Goddess of All-goodness, and every day it is my duty to show her I have been true to her name."

"What do you mean?" I asked with a tentative grin.

"Radia asks that you be what she is." I must have still looked confused because he added, "She demands I be the face of virtue. Until I uphold my oath to my goddess, that is what I will see in that mirror. A man of honour, humility, and justice. A man who is good and worthy."

"It looks like a normal mirror to me," I muttered, daring another glance at my reflection and seeing an unflattering rendition of myself scowl back at me. I hadn't detected any particular magical attribute to the mirror. Having said that, I was addled and not particularly interested in what the gods thought of me. They had never done me any favours.

"That may be so for you, Gerome. You have not chosen to make an oath to Radia." Bijan's features suddenly twisted into a mask of unease. "I, on the other hand, have sworn myself to her. My greatest fear is that one day I will fail her. That I might see someone unworthy stare back at me. So, I must strive each day to be better than the last…" His voice trailed off.

"Sounds like Radia is asking a lot of you, Bijan. People have bad days, good days, unremarkable days. You can't expect to be perfect all the time."

Bijan smiled faintly back at me. "That's what being a hero is all about."

"I'll take your word for it." I peered over my shoulder, in the direction of his tent. "Where's Najib?"

"Already in bed. My brother has had a long day."

"I hope he's okay. I take it his hand wasn't as bad as it first appeared?"

"Yes... he's feeling much better."

I did have another question that had been floating about my brain. One that I had been meaning to ask Bijan from the moment I'd met him. "If you don't mind me asking, why would two princes want to embark on a demon hunt? I doubt you'd have much use for the land, titles, and riches Brent promised us."

"It's *Lord* Brent," corrected Bijan. When he noticed my consternated expression he added, "You are correct. My brother and I are not seeking land, titles, or riches. The truth of the matter is no champion has ever defeated a demon. Najib and I will be the first. It is the final challenge the Sultan of Sipera bestowed upon us. Fulfilling our father's quest will signal our readiness to assume his mantle as rulers of Sipera."

I drew my mind back over arcane history.

Bijan was right. The Enchanted Institution, and its secretive order of special agents, always took down demons, without exception. Lots of champions had died trying though, so that should count for something.

"Cool," was all that came out of my mouth. Bijan was very pretty to look at.

There was a moment of awkward silence before he blurted out, "I do not trust our companions."

Glancing around to make sure we weren't being overheard, I whispered, "Sha-sha is terrifying, isn't she?"

From his frown, it dawned on me that he was serious.

"Not Sha-sha," murmured Bijan. "Polly."

"Where'd you get that impression?" I asked, knowing exactly from where he'd gotten that impression.

"Ever since we encountered the black pillar, I knew something was wrong with the girl." He paused, seemingly for dramatic effect. "There is an evil presence in our midst. Did you see how Polly wilfully crossed the blood circle?"

I had. But in all fairness so had Najib. It's just that Najib… was Najib.

"Agreed, there's some truth to that," I said, "but labelling Polly as downright *evil* seems like a significant overreach."

"I have a way of knowing when those who are evil lurk nearby." There was a conviction in Bijan's voice I found almost unnerving. He reached inside his silk shirt and pulled out an amulet. Attached by a metal ring to a finely crafted chain, the pendant consisted of a small, circular mirror clasped within a bronze frame. Another mirror. I shouldn't have been surprised – Radia and whatnot. It occurred to me that the amulet might have been fashioned from the missing fragment of the full-sized mirror in front of us.

"When I hold this amulet in my fist and point it at the people in my proximity, I know if there is evil in their hearts."

"This all sounds a bit reductive, Bijan. People aren't simply 'good' or 'evil'…" With a sigh, I decided to indulge him. He was even cuter when he got intense. "How accurate is this thing?"

"It might give false readings in the presence of tax collectors and red squirrels, but otherwise, it is very reliable." I watched as he clasped the pendant and stared intently about the campsite. His eyes hesitated on each of the five marquees. On Polly's, then on Sha-sha's. Then, as if following a trail of sorts, his eyes meandered towards me. He suddenly let go of the amulet. Something had changed.

"Everything okay, Bijan?" I asked.

"Yes. Nothing. All is well." The champion was looking at me like he'd never seen me before. "Must be the squirrels."

We were in a treeless, icy flat in the ass-end of nowhere. There were no squirrels. There was no life at all. A gelid rivulet of fear shot down my backbone, cleaving through the warmth of the goblin grog. I sobered up instantly. "I think we should go to bed."

"Yes," murmured Bijan. His eyes were still drilling into mine. "We should."

For a brief and tantalising moment, I thought he might invite me into his tent. However, to an equal measure of disappointment and relief, Bijan did not. A little dejectedly, I walked around the boulder and leaned against its cragged surface. Just as I was about to bring my destination into focus, an eerily familiar voice rang through my brain, shattering the relative calm I'd barely been holding together.

The champion knows...

Maybe.

We'll have to kill him.

Piss off, Al.

You don't have a choice, little man.

Last I checked, I was still in charge, Al. I'll deal with it.

I was done with this conversation. I plucked a mushroom from my pocket and downed it with practised ease. As I blinked out of existence, I thought of the way Bijan had looked at me. I almost wished I'd never reappear.

Ping.

Chapter Four

DEATH BARRIER

The following morning, I blinked back to reality in an unexpectedly good mood. It's not as if my current predicament had changed. I still looked like a reeking vagrant who'd slept in a messy hovel in no-space. I'd still lost my job. I still hadn't seen my family in ages. I was still the recipient of a dark entity that threatened to take over my body and destroy all life as we know it. I still missed Constantine…

But, all things considered, I was feeling *okay*. Which was a damn sight better than how I usually felt.

I stuffed my boots on. They were damp but I resisted the temptation to dry them by magical means. Since turning my underwear drawer to breadcrumbs in an attempt to do laundry, I'd given up on performing minor housekeeping spells; I'd been free-balling it for months. An addled brain is inept at performing errands that require a trivial amount of arcana and a pinch of self-respect. Tasks such as folding sheets and doing the dishes ended up with explosions and bystanders crying for mercy. Partridge had begged me never to help him clean up at the *Roaring Peacock* again. I had long suspected Al's chaotic energy had something to do with my inability to do anything constructive. Demons are pernicious entities hellbent on tearing, shattering, and destroying everything they can on this side of the veil. So, I was stuck with the magic that made me vanish or things go *boom*.

In a rare show of dignity, I decided that, if Bijan's mirror was still leaning on the boulder, I'd give myself a haircut. My hair hadn't been this unruly since my days as an undergraduate, living off oatmeal and sugared water.

Yet, as soon as I meandered around the huge rock, I discovered the mirror was gone. Bijan must have moved it. Before I could feel too annoyed with him, there was a petrifying scream.

"What now?" I groaned, jogging towards the source of the distress.

I wasn't alone. People were appearing from all over the encampment, half dressed and weapons in hand. The commotion had come from one of the five marquees. With a sinking sense of foreboding, I realised it was Polly's.

A crowd had already started to form, sealing the entrance of the tent from view.

"Coming through! Coming through!" Putting my size to good use, I navigated the various posteriors and thighs until I emerged at the front of the line.

My heart sank.

There was a goblin lying on a sleeping mat on the floor. Dead.

Bijan was kneeling beside the creature, inspecting the body. He was sporting the same refined, loose-fitting clothes that had flattered his figure the night before. He must have jumped out of bed at short notice. Najib was standing next to his brother, already clad in his breast-plate, gauntlets fitted, and greaves fastened around his legs, not an inch of skin showing beneath the heavy silver armour. I glanced at the imposing human and imagined Najib might be wearing a sombre expression under his helmet.

Najib spotted me and said, "Goblin is dead."

Having brought me up to speed on the obvious, the towering metal man went back to staring at the body. I noticed his hand appeared much better – well, at least, less like a poorly-fashioned club.

"Thanks, Najib." I came forward and peered over Bijan's shoulder. There was no apparent sign of injury on the corpse. No cuts or stab wounds. Not even a bruise. The goblin's eyes were shut as if he had died in his sleep. With an uncomfortable pang in my belly, I recognised him as the honoured elder, Bingop-ul. The goblin was one of the tent carriers in Polly's squadron. I knew for certain because, the night before, he'd used a tent peg to crack open the forbidden keg of booze he and the other goblins had snuck in.

Sha-sha was observing the scene from afar, like a vulture might contemplate carrion. I tried to repress the vision of her jaw unhinging to gobble up the poor Bingop-ul.

Polly, too, was standing nearby, her arms crossed and an unpleasant leer on her face. The spore-like miasma that spiralled around her person seemed even more noticeable in the light of dawn that winked through the mountain peaks.

"We should go," she whined after a minute. "We have to get to Elderstay."

A low growl came from the marquee's shadowy corner. I noticed with unease that the goblins, irrespective of their squadron, were clustered together there. They were spluttering and snarling in their native tongue, all the time glowering at the rest of us. It's remarkable how quickly people remember they belong to different species when things like this happen.

"We can't go!" sneered one. "Someone did this, yes-yes!"

"Slain he was!" cried another.

"She did it! She murdered him, she did!" A goblin was waving his finger at Polly, at a safe distance. "She murdered Bingop-ul!"

Polly's dark eyes turned slowly to the accusatory goblin behind the finger. "Careful, little goblin. I *have* killed for less."

Bijan rose to his considerable height, a measured and calm movement. All in the room went quiet, even the furious goblins. It was clear who we all thought was in charge.

"Did you do this, Polly?" he asked. Despite Bijan's suspicions about the weird girl, his tenor was not reproachful. If I were her, I would have sensed that this was my chance to come clean and be treated with mercy. My *one* chance.

"Of course I didn't!" she spat. "The goblin died in his sleep."

"No blood," said Sha-sha, in a tone that peppered my arms with goosebumps. "No bruises. Magic could. Magic spores."

Sha-sha made a valid point. I quietly contemplated Polly with the eye of an academic. If not precisely channelled or properly contained, magic could be more trouble than it was worth. Sometimes it chops firewood, ignites hearths, makes a meal, and folds the laundry. Sometimes it turns your knickers into breadcrumbs. I wondered how many of the mysterious spores her fellow tent mates had inhaled in their sleep. Death wasn't an inconceivable outcome if they had. The crux of the matter was, had it been an accident or not?

"Gerome, what do you think?"

Bijan had asked the question. I could sense the weight of his words, the gravity of his stare. Suddenly, every pair of eyes was on me.

Say it. Say it was Polly.

Go away, Al.

Let the goody-goody champion cut off her head and leave her to rot.

That gruesome image was enough to have me sweating bullets. Enough to make me speak the *words*. The words I hated the most in the entire world.

"What was that, Gerome?" asked Bijan, after my unintelligible mumble.

"I said, *I don't know*."

I could almost see the recently gained approval of my drinking buddies disappear from their faces. Bijan, too, held my gaze for longer than was comfortable before turning to the goblins. "I am profoundly saddened by your loss. I assure you we will not leave for Elderstay until Bingop-ul has been given the death rights customary to his people and due respects paid."

It was a fair statement. One which might have calmed the situation and returned some semblance of cohesiveness to our diverse and fraying group.

Polly had other plans.

"I have a better idea."

Looking back to that moment, it was the ballsiest thing I have ever witnessed. And also the nastiest.

Polly made a slicing motion with the flat of her palm. A funnel of sand-coloured dust homed in on the goblin. I watched in horror as the airborne ooze poured into Bingop-ul's parted mouth, and the gaunt creature's chest swelled with a sickly breath. Accompanied by an eerie crunching sound, Bingop-ul rose unsteadily into a standing position, lichen patterning his face and mushrooms forming misshapen growths on his swampish skin.

People screamed. Weapons were pointed and threats uttered, but none dared approach Polly or her rickety "fungified" puppet.

Bijan stood rooted to the spot. It was the first time I'd seen him hesitate. He did not know what to do. Frankly, neither did I. The only one of us who looked anything other than horrified was Sha-sha. And Najib, because it was hard to tell with the helmet on and all.

I knew very little about necromancy. It was a touchy subject in most respectable arcane establishments. What I did know was that there were a thousand regulations in place to prevent the kind of magic Polly had performed on the dead goblin. Yet, whatever she had done did not taste demonic or even nefarious exactly. This was something else, something different. Unlike the walking corpses that had plagued our journey, Bingop-ul wasn't undead. But he wasn't Bingop-ul, either. Another entity was shuffling his feet and moving his arms. I watched the spores coalesce around the girl and wondered, *what the hell are they?*

"Come on then," sniggered Polly, marching through the crowd with the bumbling Bingop-ul in tow. There was plenty of wailing and shoving in the ruckus that followed as the recruits fell over each other to put as much distance between themselves and the monstrosity and its master. "Let's get moving people. Elderstay isn't getting any closer."

It shouldn't come as a shock to anyone that of the fifty-odd people we'd started with, less than half stayed. Making obscene gestures and taking a few digs at our mothers, the goblins gathered anything they could carry – theirs or otherwise – and scarpered off into the frozen wasteland. A handful of humans from our squadrons also decided to call it quits. One of mine, too: the balding moustachioed guy who'd given me eager looks during yesterday's revelries. A pity, really. Before parting ways, he informed me he was going to retire and become a famous potter in the alternative hamlet of Lorinfale. I watched with a degree of envy as the quitters ventured into the wilderness and headed back to Snowden.

Bijan did his best to keep everyone focused and on track. But his authority had taken a devastating blow. His orders were followed with ill-disguised malcontent. The recruits needed to be told twice and, even then, tasks were performed poorly and with noticeable delay. I wasn't being particularly helpful, but neither were the other "people of talent", as Lord Brent had so optimistically called us. I glanced around to see Sha-sha on her tippy toes, peering into the grooves of Najib's helmet. Najib didn't seem to mind. I wondered if something sexual was going on between them but dismissed the idea when Najib droned, "Do not touch."

Bad luck, Sha-sha. I suspected champions took a vow of chastity while out and about adventuring. What a waste.

My eyes trailed on the two black specks at the edge of the encampment. Polly hadn't gone far. The girl was sitting outside the campsite with the dead goblin, her manner casual and unbothered, as if she hadn't just destabilised the geopolitical stability of the area and endangered the alliance between the races who jointly occupied Snowden. I wanted to dull my uneasy feelings with drugs. But, as I watched Bijan grimly oversee the lax disassembling of our encampment, something told me I needed to keep my head. If not for me, for our dejected leader.

After less than half an hour, we were somewhat packed up and ready to depart. Three of the marquees were left behind because we didn't have enough people to carry them.

We continued our journey as a single unit of sorts. One in which no one talked and everyone behaved like we were simply travelling in the same direction. The only thing we appeared to agree on was staying away from Polly and whatever Bingop-ul had become. The girl was treading ahead of us, the sad remains of the goblin stumbling in front of her like an unassuming, ghoulish bodyguard. I heard some dark mutterings from members of my squadron. Something about *slitting throats* and *sleep*, followed by a lot of ominous glares in Polly's general direction. I should have left it alone. But I couldn't help myself.

"What was all that about?" I snapped, catching up with Polly.

The girl shot me an innocent glance. "What do you mean?"

"This!" I blurted out, making wide circling motions at the undead goblin nearby. "All of this!"

"What about it?"

"You can't bring people back from the dead and cart them around like meat sacks for your own enjoyment!"

"The goblin croaked in his sleep. I don't see the problem."

If she didn't, I doubted I could explain it to her. I tried anyway.

"It's the worst form of magic!" I dropped my voice to a hurried whisper. "Spellcasters have been reported for a lot less. Do you want the Enchanted Institution after you?"

"It's not forbidden magic," said Polly, in a tone that suggested she didn't care much either way. "I didn't *resurrect* the goblin's body. I planted it. Now, instead of flesh, he has spores. Instead of blood, he has spores. Instead of bone, he has more spores. It's another kind of life."

"This isn't a gardening project, Polly!" I shook my head in dismay. "This type of stuff gets people upset."

"I don't give a damn about people."

I noticed it then, something about the way she flicked her eyes from me to her personal, mobile mushroom farm. I recognised that look. I'd worn it as well, of late. Like she was the loneliest person in the world.

"Suit yourself," I barked in frustration. "It's crap like this that gives us arcane practitioners a bad name!"

"I don't care. I just want to reach Elderstay and get this over with."

Me too. I wanted to be paid. I wanted to set off for Maracanda. I wanted to be cured. Then I wanted to spend the rest of my days at a tropical resort, sipping white wine served in crystal goblets by scantily clad pool boys.

Aside from our very own undead goblin, the way to Elderstay was corpse-free. But it was not without other hints of evil. Sound, for example, did not travel as swiftly as it should. The heavy crunching of our booted feet on snow and ice and the odd mumble among travellers made almost no audible noise. Every word felt like a whisper. Even though it couldn't be more than early afternoon, the sky had been growing several shades darker as we approached the cursed city. As if the laws that governed the material world were bending at the seams.

In a sudden flash of radiance, a mighty fortified citadel came into view. And the first sight of our main hurdle. An eerie, mustard-coloured shimmering on the horizon. The magical barrier. It enveloped the city like a dome, from the walls' foundations to the tallest turrets, rising high above the battlements and the vestiges of torn flags, which hung unmoving despite the powerful gusts billowing from the north. I spotted a once stately banner of arms, now threadbare and dulled, dangling limply from the main entrance. I identified the worn pattern as a helmet lodged between two crossed swords. The same I'd seen in Snowden on Lord Brent's breastplate; the crest of the House of Agris. We'd arrived at Elderstay, the great city trapped beneath a prison of demonic light.

"Pretty, isn't it?" said Polly, stopping in her tracks and staring in rapture at the magical dome.

Yes. It's beautiful.

"No, Polly," I murmured, a chill in my bones. "No, it isn't…"

Elderstay had been built to withstand a large-scale assault. Erected on the top of an outcrop to exploit the rocky environment's natural layout, it overlooked the rugged terrain around it like a majestic regent on a stone throne. Aside from being safeguarded behind a gargantuan wall, fifteen feet thick, the only way across the steep ravine that surrounded the city appeared to be via an arched bridge. I suspected the bridge must have been quite a feat of engineering, had it not been for years of demonic rule that were truly starting to show. One of the supporting piers had crumbled, and by the cracks in the foundations, it seemed like the others may soon follow. The bridge was now a perilous and narrow stretch of fractured rock between us and Elderstay.

The creepy yellowish barrier winked ominously in my peripheral vision from across the bridge. While tricky to ascertain through the magical haze, I would have bet my boots that Elderstay's gateway was open. We just needed to brave a crumbling bridge with no cover or hideouts, punch a hole through a demonic barrier, and voilà. We'd be inside.

I had some notion that my spellcasters had been trained to take down the barrier. The special hex Lord Brent had mentioned. I'd never bothered asking any members of my squadron what this entailed. No reason I couldn't remedy that at the eleventh hour.

"We're going to use Lord Brent's magical spell," confirmed a wrinkly woman with a plush white cloud of hair atop her head. Her name was Selma and, after a brief introduction, she'd told me she'd been a prolific swine healer before taking up Lord Brent's job offer. Minding hoof disease and piglet rashes had been her speciality.

"And what would that be?" I asked.

"He got it off some shaman or priestess, or sumthin'," said a man with a long silver beard, who'd been listening in. "Ted, by the way, sir, nice to meet ya, heard great things. Used to be a drain specialist meself. If ya dunny got clogged, I had the magic finger for it." Ted offered me a speckled hand the consistency of moist toilet paper.

"Pleasure, Ted," I stated, resisting the urge to wipe my palm on my trousers. "A shaman or a priestess, you say?" Not exactly similar vocational careers.

"Yeah, a religious folk. Wasn't clear. Anyway, the Lord got it off a *special* person."

"And will it work?"

"Positive!" piped Selma.

A tingle of suspicion crept up my spine. "How *do* you know it will work?"

Selma and Ted looked awkwardly at each other, like children caught with their hands in the cookie jar.

"Well, it ain't the first time we've dunnit," confessed Ted.

Something started making an insistent whirring sound in the back of my brain. "This isn't the first time you've taken down the barrier?"

"It wasn't for long, sir," chimed in Selma. "Just enough to get a handful of the lads in."

"What lads?"

"Scouts," said Selma. "You know, to do some snooping about before Lord Brent sent the big guns in."

"I take it the *big guns* are us?"

They nodded at me with unnerving enthusiasm.

"So, did these scouts ever come back?" I wasn't sure I wanted to hear the answer.

"A few, sir, but they weren't quite themselves."

"What's that supposed to mean?"

"Well," Ted grimaced through browning teeth. "They were dead, sir. Still walkin', sir. But 'em specific livin' qualities were gone."

"Still, they got back, sir, which is what every good scout should," said Selma, with an unwavering smile.

Finally, I did what I always should have, had I been a sensible and law-abiding wizard who valued his life and that of others, and was passionate about growing his own kale and clean-living.

"Can you show me the spell you'll use to punch a hole through the barrier?"

Selma and Ted gave me a small demonstration. When they were done, I felt nauseated to the core, and quite ready to tell Lord Brent to stuff his quest up his backside. Before I did, I had one last question for them.

"How old are you?"

The two elderly humans looked taken aback.

"Me, sir? Not that it's polite to ask. But I know you gnomes have your customs…"

"How old, Selma?" I persevered.

"If you must know, I am thirty-nine," she replied with a haughty tilt of her head.

"Bullshit," interjected Ted. "She's conscious about her age, sir. We're both forty-one, sir. Only four years to retirement," he added happily.

"You're… you're only forty-one?"

"Yes, what about it?" Selma's wrinkled features contorted into a pained grimace. "It's been a hard winter this one. My hair's gone white. My joints hurt, my back aches, and I feel tired all the time. Everyone's been saying the same. It's this bloody demon, it is!"

"No need to be like tha', Selma. The nice gnome is goin' to make it all better, get rid of this darned monster once and for all." Ted wrapped an arm around her shoulder and gave me a meaningful look. "This demon business has us all a bit outta sorts. Many who came near this place went home not quite the same. But ya powerful folk will destroy the blasted thin', won't ya, sir?"

I could not bring myself to answer.

"Thank you, Selma and Ted, you have been most helpful," I breathed, my voice faint.

I marched off to where the other people of talent were holding an impromptu meeting, close to the bridge's crossing. As I approached them, I could tell Bijan and Polly were patching things up.

"No, you idiot!" snarled Polly. "The soldiers must hold the bridge, while the spellcasters punch a hole through the barrier! We should stand back and wait until it's done."

"I don't want to risk these peoples' lives," argued Bijan, his defined cheekbones flushed with ill-suppressed anger. "The soldiers should be the ones standing back, while we lead the attack on the enemy forces ourselves! A good leader helms his army, he does not cower behind it!"

"Who cares about some stupid soldiers?" shouted Polly.

"We fight till the last drop of blood," Sha-sha said under her breath. I couldn't tell whose side she was on.

"Our situation would have been less dire," Bijan commented darkly, "had we not lost so many good recruits to your vile trickery, Polly."

"You let three go before we even left Snowden, *champion*. I was trying to bring the dead one back so the goblin could be of use. It's not my fault people got upset."

She did have a point. A sick, twisted point.

"Guys," I intervened, in what I hoped was a diplomatic manner. "Quit your bitching and listen up."

Everyone turned. Then glanced downwards, realising it was me.

"Yeah, so," I began, "I was talking with some of the recruits. This isn't the first time Brent has sent people through the barrier."

"*Lord* Brent," amended Bijan.

I noticed Sha-sha made a sudden movement, but when I looked at her, she had gone as still as a statue.

"What do you mean?" asked Polly.

"I mean, we are not the first meat sacks His Lordship sent on a suicide mission. Because this is what it is. A *suicide* mission." I took a deep breath. "I think only dead people can go through the barrier."

"What do you mean?" blurted out Bijan. The follow-up question was uttered in a slightly more threatening tone. "How do you know?"

It saddened me how distrustful he sounded. I'd been hoping the champion had forgotten about our little misunderstanding with the amulet last night.

"I've been making some inquiries and drawing some logical conclusions," I said, trying not to sound too defensive. "Those dead bodies we found at the blood circle and the ones we spotted as we crossed through the ice wall. They're coming from within Elderstay itself."

"No matter," snapped Bijan. "We will use Lord Brent's special hex to break in and end this evil!"

"Or die trying. What your dear Lord Brent failed to mention was that he'd already sent a scouting party through the magical barrier. The spellcasters managed to punch a hole in the dome, and the scouts strolled in alive but walked out dead. Those who *did* walk out, that is. But that's not the only thing bothering me. The hex to crack open the barrier… It's forbidden magic."

"What is that?" asked Sha-sha, as if the notion that certain things might be forbidden was completely novel to her.

"The evil kind. The spell to bring down the barrier doesn't destroy the demonic dome: it feeds it. If my thinking is correct, the hex overloads the barrier by funnelling a huge amount of life force to it all at once. This causes minor disruptions in the barrier's matrix. Long enough for living people to get through. As for the spellcasters, using that incantation consumes their vitality, instigating a cascade effect that leads to early decay of living matter and precocious ageing." Their blank stares confirmed what I'd often suspected about the public education system. "What I mean is, damaging the barrier sucks the life out of you."

There was a long and uncomfortable pause.

Bijan seemed to be staring down an abyss. His mood had visibly picked up since we'd reached Elderstay. Probably because of all the smiting evil he'd been hoping to do. I could tell the knowledge that his beloved Lord Brent was dabbling in forbidden magic, and the fact that taking down the barrier would harm those doing it was putting a damper on his plans for the day.

"What do we do, Gerome?" he asked, his tone almost meek. I felt oddly fuzzy that Bijan had asked me.

"We smite evil," uttered Najib in his monotone voice. After a moment, he added, "We go inside."

I opened my mouth to argue but something made me stop. Najib's gauntleted hand. It looked normal again. No indications of injury or abnormalities whatsoever.

"We have to go!" yelled Polly. She was quivering, her fingers balled into fists and her spores writhing fiercely around her arms. "We have to go right now!"

"Hey,' I interjected, looking around at the group. "Where's Sha-sha?"

There was a sudden blasting sound. A crackling of magic I was only too familiar with. We turned to the source of the commotion to see Bingop-ul staggering down the bridge in the direction of the barrier.

The undead goblin was heading straight for Elderstay.

Chapter Five

LAST WORDS

My verging-on-senile spellcasters appeared to have taken the goblin's stroll towards the cursed city as a sign. Having positioned themselves halfway up a steep, rocky slope, the old coots had begun tossing volleys at the barrier. Snaking rods of crimson light collided with the mustard-coloured forcefield, causing a rippling effect like drops in a puddle. Yet unlike the calming sound of patting rain, the noise the red rods made when they struck the barrier brought to mind puppies being strangled by a crazed raccoon. In the distance, cadaveric forms were emerging from the barrier and staggering onto the bridge. Their advance was relentless – albeit a little stiff. The remaining swordsmen and archers in our unit had their weapons cocked and ready and were looking around for some semblance of leadership.

"Were we meant to start? What should we do, sirs?" they yelled, as Najib and Bijan came running into their midst, followed shortly behind by Polly and *lots* behind by yours truly. Bijan cast his eyes about what was to be our battlefield. The spellcasters blasting shots without a clear target. A dead goblin tottering off towards Elder-stay. Malevolent bony figures flooding from the magical forcefield. The utter lack of a plan. Seemed like the job for a hero.

"Ready your weapons!" Bijan drew his sword high above his head. "For Lord Brent! For Lord Edmund! For the people of Snowden! For the people of Elderstay! For Radia!" Having exhausted his list of associates, the champion plunged his helmet over his head and launched towards the bridge. I was certain I caught the glimpse of a relieved smile on Bijan's lips before his handsome features vanished behind a layer of polished steel. There was a rousing cheer as our recruits stampeded after him. Najib, loyal to a fault and incapable of independent thought, was careening alongside his brother, brandishing his massive greatsword in both hands.

There was a *blip* as Bingop-ul vanished behind the barrier, ignored by the skeletons. At least that much of my theory was true: only the dead could cross the barrier. I heard Polly scream something at him. There was still no sign of Sha-sha.

Disgusted with everyone – and mostly with myself – I joined the spellcasters on the cliff. I sensed the heat of the destructive spells rubbing like sandpaper against their auras, grating away at the stuff that makes people alive. Talk about throwing your years away. Bijan, Najib, and Polly weren't acting much better. Gridlocked on a narrow and rickety bridge with no plan, converging on the demonic barrier as if they couldn't wait to plunge into our enemy's hands. I had to assume they had a death wish.

Bijan knows too much. It would be the perfect opportunity...

If you want me to fireball the bridge and kill everyone on it, the answer is – and always will be – "no".

You have to do something, little man.

Well, we're not doing that, asshole.

Oh well, your funeral. We could just do the other thing we do.

What?

We could go.

Go where?

Go far away. Somewhere nice. Somewhere with pool boys.

I should have realised then. If even my resident nightmare didn't want to go to Elderstay, I definitely shouldn't have. I am a little ashamed to admit I loved Al's idea of abandoning my squadron and my would-be friends. I had the prime opportunity, too. A horde of skeletons had amassed on the bridge, ready to meet my companions, and the remnants of our armed forces. The spellcasters kept firing at the barrier, oblivious to my presence.

Then it dawned on me. Al had proposed it. That's what made it wrong.

Against my better judgement, I emptied whatever was left of my red pouch into my open palm. A considerable fistful of *roard* courage. The burning in my nostrils was followed by an electric shock that crackled from the top of my skull to the very tip of my tailbone. Al's cruel whispering vanished instantly. A pleasant residual tingling coursed through my body.

Oh yeah, baby.

I have some vague recollection of rushing down the cliffside screaming like a banshee. *Duck, dodge, scoot, let me in, coming through.* Somehow, I was at the front line with the swords and the skeletons. Bolt, bolt, bolt again. My hits collided with a degree of reckless luck as bone shards ricocheted off the bridge's balustrades. I ducked under Najib's legs. I jabbed a femur. Shot a tibia. I was invincible. They couldn't stop me. No one could stop me! *Jab. Punch.* Ow, was I bleeding? Likely. I spotted Bijan cleaving through the incoming undead foes. He was so majestic. I watched in awe as he pushed through the enemy lines. *Go, you beautiful moron, go. Swing-swing, cling-clang,* skeleton bits piling on the slender battlefield. But there was no end to them. For every skeleton that dropped, three more would emerge from the barrier.

I didn't feel fatigued. I only began to realise I might be out of juice when bolts left my fingers only to plop in sad puddles of light on the stone ground. I can't remember exactly how I was dropped on my back. All I remember was the air being punched out of me.

My shoulders slammed against the unforgiving surface. Bone fingers around my neck. *Get off of me. Can't breathe. Oh, okay. Harder, daddy. Oh, no-no, too hard! What's the safe word…?*

There was a deafening rumble. Through tearing eyes, I saw a gash had opened in the barrier. My senior spellcasters had done it. With no help from me, for sure.

"Run!"

I had no idea who had spoken over the blasting and slashing of metal on flesh and bone. Bijan and Najib hurtled through the gap. Polly rushed after them, her cloud of spores leaving a tawny mist in her wake.

Darkness was edging closer on the verge of my sight. I couldn't breathe…

With a sudden *whoosh*, the skeleton who had been throttling me was projected through the air and over the balustrade. I lifted my head to see a thick greenish shape coil around my ankle. It began to drag me with purposeful might towards the chink in the barrier.

I twisted my body to grip the slippery brickwork. Nope, I didn't want to go. I didn't!

Maybe I should have accepted my fate. I would have spared myself the nightmares. Instead, I resisted whatever was drawing me to Elderstay. And bought myself enough time to witness our brutal defeat.

Cadavers in the thousands were pouring from the snowy cliffs like angry ants crawling over a chalk mound. They had followed us since the blood circle. Since the narrow passageway through the ice. Waited for us to rest and recover, and feel the illusion of safety, as we travelled to Elderstay. With the unrelenting perseverance possible only to a lifeless being. My ears filled with screams, as the undead descended upon the living.

I thought of Selma and Ted. Of retirement. Of pool boys. And my mum. She would have liked pool boys too. Lastly, I spared an instant of painful longing for Constantine. It must have been love.

Then everything went dark.

Gerome...

Uh?

Gerome, get up.

Al?

"Gerome, get up." It was an ominous, almost artificial, voice. I opened my eyes to find I was being swallowed in Najib's shadow. The darkness behind the slits of his helmet startled me. No eyes glinted back. I couldn't smell the slightest hint of perspiration coming from him. Nothing. It was too dark. Too dark…

I passed out again.

I'm not sure how long after, I felt something frigid and hard beneath my haunches. I blinked. This time, I glimpsed the familiar faces of Sha-sha, Polly, and Bijan looming over me.

"Gerome?" It was Bijan, from what seemed like a million miles away. "Please, get up. We have to go."

I doggedly refused. I wanted to stay where I was. Wherever that might be. All I could feel was the dull pounding in my head, the throbbing of my own listless heart in my ears. I was exhausted. Totally and utterly spent.

"Get up, gnome." Polly's words carved through the haze in my brain. "Or Sha-sha says she will eat you."

Well, I wasn't *that* tired.

I begrudgingly heaved myself into a sitting position before a blinding pain made me double over. I pressed my fingers against the source of the agony, and my hand came back red and sticky.

"You are hurt." It was Najib's resounding voice, in the proximity of my left earlobe. I realised the two champions were supporting me.

I heard the sound of a cork popping and breathed in a smell like chemical tar.

"You had a bone shard embedded in your chest," explained Bijan. Some small part of me was aware a gloved hand was dabbing me with something moist. "Luckily, it seems to have missed your vital organs."

I'd been annoyed at the brothers' conscientiousness when they had purchased half the apothecary's wares in Snowden. Now I just wanted Najib to hold me in his enormous, steely arms for the rest of eternity, while Bijan gently tended to my wound…

"What the hell!" I cursed, as Polly yanked me to my feet. The blotchy girl clasped a hand over my mouth.

"Shut up!" she snarled in a forced whisper. "Look around!"

Oh. So, that's what all the fuss was about.

We appeared to be in a town square. A massive fire was burning at the centre of the plaza. The blaze was as tall as a two-storey building, but it did not appear to be consuming anything. There was no wood, no coal, no nothing. Like pale, lemon-coloured tongues, the flames lapped the air. Neither the colour nor the behaviour had much in common with a normal fire, not even a magical one. It emitted no heat, no real light, either. That came from the mustardy glow of the barrier above our heads. Around the fire walked people. Dead people. Dragging their feet along the ground, like puppets on short strings.

"They haven't made a move towards us yet," said Bijan. He had removed his helmet. His thick hair was matted and a trail of dried blood painted one side of his face.

The others didn't look much better.

Polly had a deep gash over one eye and bad bruising down her arms. Najib was sporting a few dents in his breastplate and a noticeable depression on the top of his helmet. The only one who appeared unscathed was Sha-sha.

"By the way, where were you back there, Sha-sha?" I scolded the woman, remembering the conspicuous absence of a giant snake during our skirmish on the bridge.

Sha-sha assessed me with a slight curl on her thin lips. Like a python might evaluate an annoyingly talkative piglet in light of how widely it'd have to extend its jaw to swallow the creature. I must have looked like quite the snack. Someone had ripped open my coat and shirt to medicate my chest injury, and half of my buttons were missing. I was prepared to drop the subject, but Bijan put a hand on Sha-sha's shoulder and mine in an unsolicited conciliatory gesture.

"Gerome," he began, in a patronising tone that made me want to slap him. "Sha-sha was the one who rescued you. She tossed aside the skeleton that had you pinned down and dragged you inside."

"Oh." I flushed. That explained the green thing that had me by the ankle. "Sorry. I guess."

Sha-sha's ominous scrutiny didn't end there. I felt a nip of cold on my exposed skin which couldn't be attributed solely to Elderstay's cool and unfriendly climate. I'd have to magic myself away to no-space tonight.

"So," I said, trying to pull the ribbons of my tattered robes over my bandaged chest, "I was a little distracted at Brent's briefing. After we break through the barrier and enter the city, did he add anything else?"

"It's *Lord*—"

"Such as?" Polly asked before Bijan could finish.

"Did Brent hint at where we should start once in Elderstay? Or tell us more about what awaits us, perhaps?"

"A demon awaits us, dummy," stated Polly, ostensibly unfazed at the prospect.

"I'd gathered as much," I snapped, glowering at the girl with unabated frustration. "But surely, Brent must have given us a few more details? Anything at all?"

"No more details," added Najib, equally unperturbed.

"So, this is it? The five of us waltzing into an abandoned stronghold to defeat a demon? With no plan or information whatsoever?"

"The six of us," corrected Polly. Bingop-ul made a wheezy sound from a darkened corner by the gateway as if answering a school roster. His features resembled mushroom puree at this stage.

"Do not fear, Gerome. We have the All-good Radia on our side and brave hearts beating in our chests. With allies such as these, we cannot fail!" Bijan's tone was enthusiastic but his gaze did linger on a few elements in our party, dead goblin included. I suspected it was taking all of his chivalry not to single out Polly and Bingop-ul from his assertion.

"We will win," said Najib. It dawned on me then that every time I heard the armoured wardrobe of a man speak, it was in no more than three-word sentences. Such a specific speech impediment, it had to be intentional. Or some kind of arcane curse or magical accident. Or a weird oath to a deity of conciseness.

"So, that's it? *Lord* Brent didn't give you any more intel?" I glanced between the champion brothers, seeking some semblance of reason. "Doesn't anyone else find this whole mission a bit haphazard?"

"We trust His Lordship's noble intentions," declared Bijan, forever protective of our aristocratic employer. "Lord Brent wishes to free Elderstay from its plight for the safety of the people of Snowden and surrounding territories. After all, Lord Edmund was his brother. It is Lord Brent's bloodright to avenge the death of his kin. There is no greater privilege than to lend our aid in a quest as righteous as this one."

I'd heard this warm and fuzzy bullshit before. But not the part about the former Lord of Elderstay.

"I can't recall Lord Brent saying Lord Edmund was his brother," I mumbled.

"It is a sore point," said Bijan.

"Enough of this!" Polly smacked the flat of her hand against a torch holder affixed to the wall. Red seeped from beneath the gauze around her injured wrist, her recent wound reopened. "We have to complete the mission! Destroy the demon! Gather our reward!" I don't think I'd ever seen her so upset. "WE HAVE TO GO NOW!"

The girl was loud. Too loud. We peered about with unease, but the undead prowling the plaza did not appear to have heard us. They were either deaf or they were minding their own business.

"Okay," I conceded before anyone – mainly myself – got hurt. "Let's go."

I waited for the others to precede me. When I was certain no one was looking, I dug my fists into my pockets. My hands came back empty. My three pouches. I'd lost them. No matter, I still had a few of Polly's orange mushrooms. I patted myself down, seeking the tell-tale soft bulges in my clothes…

Oh, no.

A kind of fear I'd rarely felt poured over me like ice water. The mushrooms weren't there. They must have dropped out of my coat during the battle.

"Gerome, what are you doing?" Bijan had turned back. From his tone, I could tell he thought I'd gone peculiar. I'm sure it looked that way. My eyes sprung wide in panic, my lips trembling but no words coming out, searching every inch of my person in what must have appeared like a terrible case of fleas.

I couldn't confess. I couldn't tell Bijan what was wrong. He would kill me.

"I'll be right with you!" I stammered, sweat pearling my forehead. "I just lost my… keys."

Bijan nodded as if that was a perfectly reasonable explanation for my behaviour. He joined the others who had begun to tread with care around the roaring, yellow fire, weapons at the ready.

Uh-oh.

Please, Al…

What are you going to do now, little man?

I'm begging you!

How do you plan on stopping me...

Please don't!

... from destroying the world?

His laughter echoed through my mind, and I knew. I didn't have much time.

I was a ticking bomb.

I can confidently say that, not even in my most hungover, drug-addled, and enfeebled states, have I ever moved as slowly as I did this day. Everywhere we went, lumbering corpses lurked about. The only source of light was the yellowish glint of the barrier which bathed the whole city in a wicked, suffused glow. In every alleyway, every corner – dark or otherwise – the dead crawled on whatever limbs they had left, across Elderstay's lifeless streets and tight cobbled alleys. At first, we ventured around them with great caution, our heads darting about in fear they might gang up on us all at once. But the more we inched through the city, the more we came to realise its taciturn inhabitants were not a threat. Nor were they doing much other than moving about at random. The dead did not make sounds exactly. After all, the bits associated with speech had decayed years before. But they did make a distinctive grinding noise as their bones mashed together while they moved. One I would never be able to forget.

I tried not to focus for too long on any one of the walking bodies. I could not afford my overactive imagination to tell me their stories. I attempted to ignore the gold of wedding bands, winking on their gaunt fingers. Or the smaller skeletons with school bags still slung across their sunken shoulders. Though I couldn't quite help myself tearing up at the sight of a formless mass of hair and bone curled up in wait, beside a rusted, empty bowl.

What sickened me, Al revelled in. I could sense his dark presence in my mind, swelling like a balloon in my lungs, one cloying breath at a time. Every hour, I knew there would be more of him and a little less of me. All the time, his manic smile tugged at the corner of my lips, as he delighted in the turpitude of this place.

Bingop-ul was the only member of the party that seemed to fit in. Polly's victim was doddering ahead of us, clearly in his element. We had just ducked past a street sign for an alleyway named *Periwinkle Lane*, when we spotted signs of life. Or not.

BANG. BANG. BANG.

I peered from behind the bend to see a skeleton on a doorstep, banging its head against a closed door. This must have been going on for some time, given the pronounced indentation in the wood where its skull had repeatedly collided with the solid timber.

"Well, that's not disturbing at all," I whispered with a sardonic grin.

"Let's see what it's after." Before anyone could stop her, Polly rushed from behind the corner and propelled a jet of spores at the unsuspecting skeleton. Coiling tendrils of mist grappled its limbs and pulled with vicious force. The undead thing tore into a dozen pieces.

"Striking an enemy in the back, Polly," said Bijan, sheathing his greatsword, "is not particularly *fair*."

"Fighting fair is for morons. We don't have time to waste." Polly stepped over the skull.

I noticed, with a degree of unease, that its head was still rolling about as if wanting to resume where it had left off.

As soon as the door swung open, a wall of stench struck our unwary nostrils. The smell was so revolting, I retched for a whole minute on the ingress. In the middle of the devastated and bloodied room was a body in the early stages of decomposition. Through watery eyes, I registered there were no flies – no insects of any kind – to aid the process. Life, all life, had abandoned this place. I took an educated guess at the dead human's former identity.

"Brent's scouts," I murmured, poking my head through the doorway, before ducking back out for fresh air.

"It's *Lord* Brent," griped Bijan. He began to mumble under his breath, a hand clasped around his amulet in what I assumed was a prayer. "Could you please search the body, brother?"

"Search the body," repeated Najib, bumbling towards the rotting corpse, as if he'd just been asked to assemble his favourite niece's rocking horse. The armoured champion's heavy hands started prodding and palming the body.

"Any idea what happened to the poor bastard?" I asked, trying my best to ignore the squelching sounds coming from Najib's general direction.

"What d'you think?" teased Polly. "The demon did it."

The girl was sweeping the area, nicking anything easy to pocket. I doubted there was any stuff of value. The place looked like it may have, once upon a time, been someone's living room. Now, it might have been someone's living room after a tornado had swept through it. The wallpaper had been torn and was donning dark, unidentified spatters. Pieces of furniture had been tossed aside or overturned, and the floor was soft beneath our feet, courtesy of the caved-in ceiling. I tried not to stare too long at Sha-sha. She was tasting the air with eager flicks of her forked tongue. She may very well have saved my life, but I could not shrug off the feeling she was enjoying this. All of it.

Najib finally stood, a piece of stained parchment in his hand. "A letter, brother," he said with a tone of complete indifference.

"Gerome," called Bijan, after a moment of staring at the parchment. "Would you mind reading it?"

The request surprised me, but I guessed the champion wanted to keep me involved. Or Bijan enjoyed bossing me around to feel like he was in charge. Regardless, I begrudgingly took the fetid letter from Najib, my sleeve pressed over my mouth.

"What does it say?" asked Bijan.

"It's got – ew, gross – blood all over it," I squinted. "Okay, it says: My name is…"

My name is Bellamy Kirt and I'm the body on the floor. If you're reading this, you're probably next.

Strong start. The crimson full stop added a petrifying *je ne sais quoi* to the missive. I would have been quite happy to put the letter down, but my companions were looking at me expectantly.

FYI, if you would like pen and paper for your last will and testament, I left some in the desk drawer. I'm guessing that, like me, you've been promised a hefty reward by that pompous, upper-class tosser, Brent.

I glanced up at Bijan to see his handsome features scrunched up in a constipated frown. "Oh, sorry, I meant *Lord* Brent."

"Just keep reading," said Bijan.

If at all interested in the fate of BLUE SCOUTING SERVICES LTD (for all your intelligence-gathering needs, no recon too far or too fickle), please see my report enclosed.

Well, I counted myself moderately intrigued. I turned to the next page.

DATE: Monday, 7th of Joypan, 1213 SD.
SIZE OF PATROL: 3.
NAMES: Bellamy Kirt (TL), Sam Bowman, George Figgis.
TERRAIN: Urban landscape
MISSION SUMMARY:
Day one — The spellcasters tore a hole in the Elderstay barrier at first light. Scouting Services

LTD entered Elderstay. We were told to reconvene at the gated entrance on the third day at noon. Enemy dead detected. Seemed friendly and left us unharmed. Explored the western side, but nothing to̶ We stayed in a vacant house at 54 Bayley Road for the night.

Day two – We proceeded to explore the northern suburb. Aside from continued undead sightings, little of note. Stayed in a wine cellar at 12 Minkins Lane.

Day three – Bloody typical̶ Things were going smoothly in this hellhole. At least until Sam came back from recon, begging us to go check out Lighthelm Cathedral. His lips looked dark. I assumed it'd been the wine̶ He said we should go when we didn't, Sam went mad. He stabbed me. The undead started hunting us down. got George. Reached rendezvous point before noon. Brent was a no-show.

Day four – Hiding in the house at 34 Periwinkle Lane. The dead are scratching at the door. I barricaded myself inside.

Day five – Still hiding. Still scratching. The wound doesn't stop bleeding. I ran out of food.

Day six – Still nothing. They won't let me sleep. The wound is going septic. Ran out of water.

Day seven – Brent was meant to open the barrier at noon̶ days ago. I can hear them clawing through the walls. I haven't slept in so long. Think

I'm imagining things. Last night I thought I heard music from ▓▓▓▓▓▓▓ I might just open the door and get this over with...

With a shiver, I realised he must have. While it was hard to tell, the man's wounds did seem to be concentrated on his chest and face, as if he'd confronted whatever had killed him head-on. We hadn't found Mr Kirt far from the door. I glanced down at the final scribble at the end of the letter.

FINAL OBSERVATIONS: Gemma, I loved you. To my brother, Percy, I know the kid is yours. Take good care of them for me, you asshole.

That was it. The last words of Bellamy Kirt. I noticed a round stamp embossed on the bottom of the letter. A blue horsehead. *Blue Scouting Services LTD*.

I folded the reeking pieces of parchment and carefully tucked them in my boot. I decided I would have liked Mr Kirt. His handwriting had been neat. Presumably a requirement of his job, with sending legible missives from the enemy lines and all. I glanced down at the man's body and made a quiet vow of my own. That I'd not have to use the pen and paper he'd referred to. Or meet a fate as abysmal as this one.

Better things await us, Gerome. If you would just let me take the lead.

I tightened my fists, magic crackling around my knuckles. *I will never let you lead!*

"The name of this place Mr Kirt mentioned: *Lighthelm*," mused Bijan, the sound of his voice drawing me back to the present. "I have heard that name before…"

"Duh, it's after Agris of the Lighthelm!" growled Polly, an ugly sneer warping her already hostile expression. "Don't you know? He was an old folk hero with a magic helmet called the Lighthelm. An ancient god gifted it to Agris after putting a piece of its own divine essence inside it! For centuries, the Lighthelm was passed down the bloodline. From father to son." Her voice had dropped to a barely audible mutter.

"Ah, yes. Agris. The founder of Lord Brent's family line." Bijan nodded to himself.

"And Lord Edmund's!" snapped Polly.

Perhaps it was my imagination, but I sensed the girl was more combative than usual. And since when did she know so much about obscure stories regarding aristocratic lineages?

"How do we proceed?" asked Sha-sha, interrupting their exchange with a hiss that sent creepie crawlies down my spine.

"We must go to Lighthelm Cathedral," declared Bijan.

"Sounds like that is where the trouble started," I began, but I'd seen that expression on Bijan's face before. "Fine, we go to the cathedral. But can we at least head there in the morning? When we are refreshed and medicated?"

And by "medicated", I didn't just mean a change of bandages. Polly had to have more mushrooms. She was made of mushrooms. I needed to get her on her own, away from prying ears.

Bijan's gaze darted through the door to the sky outside. It was hard to tell the time due to the barrier's ever-glowing, sickly tinge. But it had to be bedtime by now. My crankiness suggested as much.

"We will need our strength for the battle ahead," agreed Bijan, a small frown line appearing between his eyes. "Maybe we can stay here for the night—"

"Not here!" I snapped. "We find a tavern or a hostel. Somewhere that doesn't reek of the poor bastard your Lord sent to die."

Bijan opened his mouth and then must have thought better of it. "Very well."

I let the others go first before walking to the overturned desk. I pulled open the stiff drawer with some difficulty. Mr Kirt had been true to his word. I folded away a few pieces of parchment and took the pen. Just in case.

That's when I noticed Sha-sha was still in the room with me. Alone.

Without so much as a gulp, I dashed outside as fast as my legs would carry me. I waited between Najib's towering presence and the wonky Bingop-ul. Sha-sha stayed behind. She returned a moment later, licking her lips. Her belly looked swollen.

No one dared ask why.

Chapter Six

PLAY OUR SONG

If this was to be my last night among the living, I was not about to settle for the first stable or swine pen we came across along the way. Bijan tried to duck into a couple of grubby hovels, but I kept marching on. And I intended to keep going until I stumbled upon a place commensurate with my yearning for a pinch of grandeur in life. Constantine used to say it was how I made up for my stature. My heart's desire appeared in the form of a double-storey brick building, a few hundred feet from the home in which we had found Bellamy Kirt's body.

There was a promising sign hanging from the entrance.

"The *Gallant's Rest*," I read aloud. "She's not as fancy as the *Roaring Peacock*, but it'll do for the night. Najib, if you'll do us the honours…"

"Stay back, everyone," bellowed Najib.

I moved aside, as he pounded open the huge wooden door with his ham-like fist.

We stepped inside to find a generous dining area with several round tables set at comfortable intervals around the room. From the expensive finishes on the ceiling and a glance at the dusty wine selection behind the counter, I could tell it must have been a rather stylish setting for the locals to spend an afternoon of boozing and bar fights. The *Gallant's* air was thick and musty but no one had died here. At least, not recently. Unlike the devastated house we'd left earlier, almost all of the furniture appeared to be intact. Many of the chairs had been knocked over and the tables were askew, possibly shoved aside by people in a rush, but nothing was broken. As I stepped with caution through the creaking dining area, I expected to see more borer holes in the floorboards and cobwebs among the rafters. Then, I remembered nothing had survived Elderstay. Not the spiders. Not the borer beetles. Nor the wood termites. Most definitely not the patrons.

To my relief, there were no ambling dead people about. Aside from Bingop-ul, who was attempting to climb on top of the bar counter.

"Come down, before you hurt yourself," called Polly, a curl on her lips.

I watched as the girl supported the monstrosity she'd created as it tottered along the bench. She was much nicer to Bingop-ul dead than she would ever have been to the goblin alive. Polly appeared to be far more at ease with the lifeless than the living. Less challenging, I guess.

"We should sleep together," Bijan commented suddenly.

I turned my head so fast a nerve pinched. "What?"

"On the ground floor, for protection," he continued. "We will also need to take turns keeping watch tonight, in case our enemy chooses to attack us."

"Oh yes, of course. In the same room. *Together*." I spun around to straighten some chairs and conceal my flaming face. Bijan didn't seem to have noticed my impropriety. He and Najib were far too busy clearing out a space for us in the middle of the dining area and barricading the entrance with overturned tables.

You like him.

No. Hardly.

You cannot hide from me, little man.

He has a nice smile. And a firm butt. That's all.

It doesn't ever go well for you, Gerome. Liking people. Loving them...

I'm not about to take romantic advice from a demon.

We know only too well how easily the things you love can be lost...

Just go back to whatever cesspit you crawled out of, Al.

Suit yourself. Maybe, when I take your body, I'll rip his to ribbons. Spare you the pain.

There it was. The feeling of being stifled by a crowd of giants. True, everyone was a giant to me. But in this particular crowd, a little at a time, I am shoved, nudged, and pushed, until I'm outside the gathering looking in – exiled from my own mind. Al was constricting my space, steering my thoughts to the ones he wanted me to think. The emotions he wanted me to feel. To make more of him than me. I needed something, anything, *badly*. I eyed the bottles of wine lining the shelving behind the counter. I was tempted. But I became a dangerous cocktail of scrappy and self-loathing when I was drunk. As Partridge, my innkeeper friend, could attest after spending an afternoon patching up the wall when another customer sat on my favourite barstool. I turned to look for Polly, but she was no longer helping Bingop-ul along the benchtop.

I heard a note. A piano key.

She had sat at a bench in front of a sprawling grand piano. The magnificent instrument had gone unnoticed in the dark, tucked in a recess in the wall. Its keys, covered in over a decade of dust and grime, were hard to tell apart. I watched as she pressed down on a few. The sound hung in the air and rang through the silent inn.

I knew everything about music but very little about *making* music. It was a gnome thing. I came from a long line of talented musicians – bassists, cellists, flautists, drummers, composers, singers, you name it. Every one of my brothers had mastered a musical instrument. The oldest of us, Damian, was a renowned violinist in Underdwell.

I was the exception. In my youth, I had dabbled in singing as a choir boy in a local church. I'd looked great in a dress, but I'd been kicked out after I made the head priestess weep in exasperation. Good thing I was born with a penchant for the arcane or I would have been relegated to the role of sad ginger middle-child. That position fell to Cowley, my eighth brother.

I approached Polly. We were out of earshot from the others. I noticed her smooth features were scrunched up in a look of frustrated effort, as if she was trying to remember something vitally important.

"Polly, girl, how are you doing?" I began, in what I assumed was an acceptable way to initiate a conversation with young people these days.

No answer.

"You know those mushrooms you gave me? The little orange ones? I need more. I don't have the cash right now but all things going to plan, we'll soon be loaded—"

"Not now." She was glaring at the piano, her fingers clenched so tight around the keys, her knuckles seemed on the verge of bursting through her skin. "Later."

I wanted to say that "later" may be *too* late. But the girl appeared so flustered, I decided to drop the subject. For now.

Just as I was about to turn away, I heard Polly whisper, a twinge of distress in her voice. "Our song… What was our song…? How did it go…?"

"Right," called out Bijan, his hands on his hips in a look that I found vaguely reminiscent of my mother. "Everyone, get some rest. I'll take the first watch. Polly, you'll take the shift after mine. Then Gerome. Sha-sha will take the last."

"Yes, Mum," I muttered. Fancy Al thinking I could have feelings for the bossy meatloaf.

Though Bijan had constructed a makeshift enclosure, using upturned tables and chairs to form an open space in the centre of the tavern, we weren't having any of it. To his disappointment, no one settled in the vacant patch. Polly slunk off to a far corner, not far from the piano. Bingop-ul was standing guard over her, his mouth wide open, emitting a shallow, raspy sound. I watched as Sha-sha simply lay on the floor, under a table. I suspected she needed to sleep off the poor scout. Which was good for me, since I was not sure about the status of our fraying relationship. But I was willing to bet it fell somewhere between *moderately bad* and *possible murder*. Najib had vanished. I hadn't noticed him leave. For a man his size, clad in metal from head to toe, Najib was so quiet he could go unnoticed in an empty room. People would assume he was one of those decorative armours rich nobles have lined up along their more frequented corridors. It occurred to me that I had never seen Najib without his helmet. Or seen a strip of bare skin, for that matter. Yet, unlike me after climbing a short flight of stairs, he didn't seem to sweat. Even the perfect Bijan whiffed a bit after a day cooped up in the armour. Perhaps Najib's was airtight. The lack of oxygen would have explained his sluggish mind and meek demeanour.

These were all good questions. Questions I really should have dwelt on.

I didn't. I curled up on myself behind a reclined chair and blinked myself out of existence.

Except, I didn't.

The distinctive *ping* sound the universe made to re-adjust itself to my absence when I departed to no-space, never came. I shut my eyes tight and tried again. And again. It soon became apparent I wasn't going anywhere. I brought my knees to my chest and wrapped my hands around my trembling self. I couldn't stop shivering. I wasn't cold. Nor was I frightened, exactly. It was the quaking of my addicted brain, longing for the substances I had so liberally fed it. I had fought the feeling off for as long as I could. Witches and wizards were nothing if not diligent. The concentration and focus employed in the tedious learning of the arcane could be just as efficiently converted to suppressing standard humanoid needs: the craving for food, drink, or the warmth of another in our arms. I hadn't felt the withdrawal symptoms sneak up on me until I had time to *think*. Think about how much I wanted a line of *yaydust*. How much I would have given for a mushroom morsel.

I pressed my head against my knees to stifle the sobs that I could no longer subdue.

Almost mine, little man. Almost mine...

I'd never killed. But I would have killed for it to end. Killed to not feel the way I did right then.

As it turned out, I would take a life tonight.

Music. There was music. My eyes opened to a suffused, rust-coloured glow, drifting about the ceiling. Spores. Luminescent spores pulsed in the darkness, dancing to the tune like fireflies in a field under a moonless sky. I half lifted my aching bones into a sitting position. The timber flooring that had served as my unforgiving bed mat for the night was sticky – a trademark of any self-respecting inn. I turned my stiff neck to see Polly on the piano stool. Her scabbed fingers swayed over the keyboard. The music grew like a living thing, filling every gap in the *Gallant's Rest*. The melody seeped into my bones and picked at my heartstrings. I got up with a slow and measured movement – afraid to break Polly's almost fervent concentration. I approached her silently from behind and watched, transfixed, as her fingers scurried like spiders across the ivories. Fast, almost crazed, seeking something in between the notes, as she played them. Then, the rhythm slowed almost to a standstill, and a mellow, nostalgic mumble rippled through the air, dredging up every painful feeling I had ever experienced. I couldn't stop thinking about Pringle, the pet hedgehog I had as a child.

It was a strange thing to witness. The girl who'd seemed so detached and callous, playing the piano in a way that made parts of me melt and reform, never quite the same.

A single tear lined the side of her face. There was a pause. Her fingers stopped playing. But the music continued.

"Polly, are you okay?" I asked with a shiver in my voice.

"Gerome, I was hoping you'd hear the music."

She rose from her seat, spores drawing coppery rivulets around her limbs. I watched as she pulled her hands away from the piano keys. Yet the music went on. Polly turned to face me and I jumped back in horror. As she moved out of the way, I'd seen it. A shadow perched on the stool where the girl had been sitting moments before. I did not know what I was staring at. It was draped in ribbons of darkness, swaying gently in the windless room. A chill coursed through my veins. It reminded me of the shrieking nightmare that had emerged from the obsidian pillar, back in the blood circle we'd encountered not far from Snowden.

"W-who is that?"

I felt my blood go cold as I gathered more details of the strange presence. The creature was not seated. It was hovering. The bottom half of its body was missing from the waist down. All the best parts of one's anatomy.

"Polly, what is going on?"

"Gerome," she said, her tone one of feigned kindness. "Do not be scared."

Those are the kinds of statements that elicit the exact opposite of what they are meant to accomplish. And I was scared. Very scared.

I felt the heat building in my hand. The blaze of a bright-bolt charged up my index finger until the pressure became uncomfortable beneath my nail. Who I was planning on directing all this destructive energy towards, was yet to be decided.

The music stopped. The creature turned towards me, peeling itself from the bench stool and soaring inches short of the ceiling. *Flying, huh?* A power move every spellcaster aspired to be able to perform. Lifting off the ground while blasting shots from your hands was an arcane practitioner's wet dream. It required immense discipline and a touch of madness. A fine balance between conflating magical currents. To get it wrong, by even a smidgen, would mean plunging to your death or blowing yourself up.

I watched as the thing basked in the brownish tinge of Polly's luminescent spores. I couldn't taste strawberries. Yet whatever the shadow was, it sure as hell wasn't *natural*.

"Leave, or else," I growled, pointing my weaponised finger at the billowing threads of darkness that made up the levitating monstrosity.

"Don't!" Polly cried, casting her own body between my blazing finger and the hovering eyesore. She grabbed my firing arm.

"Polly, don't be stupid!"

Her nails dug into my flesh. "It's my father!"

I dropped my hand, the potential energy draining from me faster than milk from a cow's teat.

"Your... father?"

Well, that explained a lot. Of course the despicable girl had some fiendish meddling in her hereditary makeup. But also, it explained practically nothing. I cast my eye once more over the shadow. I wasn't entirely sure what I was looking at.

"That *thing* is your father?"

"He didn't always look like that!" snarled Polly, still holding me.

I broke free from her grasp. "Polly, you need to tell me what is going on right now! Or I will wake up the others. And I will tell Bijan you've been cavorting with demons. And what do you think the *holier-than-though* champions will do?! I might even tell him about Bingop-ul. You and I both know he didn't simply die in his sleep…"

"They don't matter. None of them matter. Only you matter. You must come with us, both of you."

"Both of us?"

"I know what you're hiding, Gerome. I know about your demon. I need you both."

The secret for which I had lost my job, my apartment, my family, and my lover. The secret that had derailed my existence and dragged me onto a monochromatic path of misery, addiction, and – inevitably – my own untimely death, was out.

The feeling was strange. Relief, at first. Then fear. Fear of what her words had meant.

"What do you mean, you need us *both*?" I stammered.

Her inky black eyes set on mine, unblinking. They glowed with fanatical determination, yet, beneath it all, I detected a hint of sorrow. In that moment, I realised how young she was. A girl whose life had demanded that she grow up too fast. And, yes, Polly was human. One who had been altered and warped beyond recognition.

"You must come with us," she said, a flick of her chin directing me towards the door.

"Us?"

As if on cue, I felt Al swell inside my mind.

Things are getting interesting...

I looked around for help. I couldn't believe the others hadn't woken up yet. We weren't exactly being quiet. Something was wrong. Sha-sha, Bijan – they were very still. My heart stopped.

"D-did you kill them?"

Polly said nothing.

"Enough questions, Gerome." She extended an arm level with my face, spores swaying around her limbs.

I readied myself to fight. Then, her palm opened and all my resolve drained away.

She was holding out a single orange mushroom for me to take.

That's the problem with addicts. I would have sold an orphan to a cannibal if I knew it'd buy me an ounce of *yaydust*.

I'd started experimenting with substances because it was the only thing that prevented Al from taking over my body. Now, it was more than that. I *needed* the chemicals. And the more I did, the less I liked what I'd become. As an addict, I was the guy who pinched coins from blind beggars. Stole from Partridge's till, knowing full well he was saving for his son's education. Fudged his tax returns. And, worst of all, performed questionable acts of magic for equally questionable people, like some cheap arcane prostitute. Hence my current predicament. Of course, I'd drawn the line at forbidden magic. Just because the Enchanted Institution scared me as much as Al did.

As I reached out to grab the mushroom, she snatched her hand away.

"Come with me, Gerome, and I will give you what you need."

I gave one last desperate look around the room, seeking someone – anyone – who might stop me. In that moment, I caught my reflection in the far end of the room. There was a mirror, leaning against the wall. I hadn't noticed it before. It looked familiar, but I was too distressed to dwell on it.

As I contemplated my own reflection – a bedraggled, red-headed gnome wearing the expression of someone who was utterly done with the burden of living – I knew. That gnome was all that stood between a demon and the end of the world.

I didn't like those odds.

"Let's go."

Go on, little man. Don't keep us waiting...

I hadn't even asked where we were going.

Back outside, in the sickly yellow glow, I dragged my feet along the sullen streets of the dead. Polly's so-called "father" was floating in mid-air, leading the way. In the magical dome's mustardy light, I'd been able to gather more horrifying particulars as to our nightmarish airborne tour guide. I was almost certain the creature that hovered before me had been human once. The half of him that was left, at least. As for the devastating injury that had severed Polly's father clean in half, it seemed unlikely he'd be able to tell me about it, had I felt inclined to ask. The shadow's mouth was agape in a look of startled surprise, and I doubted there was anything but quiet decay between his chipped ivory teeth. The floating, mangled body would have been hard to tell apart from the other animated corpses wandering about Elderstay, yet – unlike the others we'd seen – this creature appeared to have some semblance of purpose.

"Uuuuuhhh…"

Polly's father wasn't the only undead I had to contend with. Bingop-ul was wheezing down the nape of my neck. The goblin was shadowing me so closely, he kept brushing up against my clothes leaving rust-like streaks on my already scruffy coat.

Polly was sauntering a few steps ahead of us, a gleeful spring in her steps. She cast the occasional glance back to check I hadn't made a run for it. Easier said than done. My hair lifted as another waft of spores came zipping past my scalp. The tawny particles were rotating in dense concentric circles around Polly, Bingop-ul, and myself. The spores appeared to be acting like some kind of shield. Not unlike the one Polly had used to protect herself when we'd fought the shadow in the blood circle. Again, I wondered about the spores' magical nature. They had been proven to counter arcane forces. Even so, a well-aimed bright-bolt might be able to blast through them…

Bah. The truth was, I was in no mood for a fight. I assumed Polly knew this. Or she wouldn't have been standing this close to a wizard who penned an academic paper entitled, *Majoris Sphaera Ignis – from Weapon of Mass Destruction to Artisanal Bread Baking: Practical Applications of Fireballs in the Modern Era.*

While the presence of the undead fungus goblin, the psychotic spore girl, and half a father figure should have been at the forefront of my worries, they didn't even make the top five. The relentless incoming darkness was ramming at the fortress of my fraying mind. I could feel Al bloating inside me, pressing against every part of my skull until I thought my head might explode.

You cannot hold me for much longer.

It was more than a threat. It was a promise.

"Polly!" I cried, in a pitiful moan. "I need that mushroom! Please, I'm begging you!"

"Almost there," she replied, a playful grin parting her lips. She taunted me, rolling the orange nugget around her palm, as if I were an unruly puppy on a leash. One that didn't deserve his treat yet. She'd make me work for it.

I like her.

I don't.

The gash on my chest ached something fierce. I wondered if my wound was getting infected. The irony of it all almost made me chuckle out loud. *Oh, let's hope that doesn't kill me…*

Does it hurt?

Like you care? Of course it hurts!

Good. You deserve the pain, little man. Do you have any idea how bored I've been?

He laughed. A slow, manic laugh that started in the depths of some unfathomable darkness, before rising up my throat and escaping in a stifled gasp from my lips.

When I finally take over your precious body. When at last I come into my own, you will see… Pure hearts will be sliced open and from their blood shall spill the New Dark…

Please stop.

…The world will live a thousand winters and taste nought but loss and misery, the silence of ten billion dead…

His voice had changed. It froze the blood in my veins. How close he was now, how loud…

…But first I'll check that wound.

Yeah. It could go septic. You don't want it going septic.

No. I do not. That would be a real bummer.

Is that because you have nothing, or, better, no one to anchor you here, Al? Without me? Without my body? Where will the Harbinger of the New Dark go… without me?

I will not fall for your petty tricks, little man! You're not the only anchor to this world. There are plenty of bad people out there. I'm sure I would find someone better. Maybe someone taller.

Before being forced back to the Shade Planes? I doubt it.

I was teasing him but an idea had occurred to me. One I'd had more times than I care to admit. And quietly filed in the most unfrequented corners of my brain as a notion I might explore – *once* all other avenues have been exhausted. But I was running out of options. True, there was a tiny chance, still a chance, that I'd somehow liberate Elderstay. Get paid. And head off to Maracanda for the fabled demon-eradicating cure.

But now, I wasn't so sure there was time for Maracanda. Time at all.

Ending your life would be pointless. And nothing more than a minor inconvenience. Anyway, you're too much of a coward.

Al was referring to the time I had tried to bright-bolt my brains out. After a glut of bad news and a heavy session of day drinking, I had brought a shaky index to my head. The thing is, magical bolts and alcohol don't mix. The shot intended to end my miserable existence had flown past my ear and hit the chandelier instead. The innkeeper's crystal pride and joy had come crashing down in the middle of the *Roaring Peacock's* bar area. Thankfully, it was early morning. At the time, the establishment had only been occupied by the regular corner boozers and the resident rat we knew affectionately as Plague. But it had taken a lot of grovelling with Partridge once I sobered up. I hadn't had the moxie to try again.

So, what's going to be of me, when you take over? What of my mind?

I'll keep you around. As a pet, perhaps. I would like you to witness the apocalypse you helped bring about. It would be - what do you people on this side call it? - a "fitting" end.

Great. Thanks. A sudden glimmer of realisation ignited my mind. *What about this other demon in Elderstay? The one that made all this mess? Are you all on the same page about the world-destroying thing?*

We all want chaos.

So, you're not worried about this other resident fiend? I paused our telepathic communication before adding, *What if this demon is more powerful than you are?*

When Al spoke next, I could almost sense his red-hot rage blast through my neural pathways.

No one is more powerful than me! No one! Not this so-called demon of Elderstay. Not this foolish girl and her spores. Not that green-skinned snake woman with the funny haircut. Not even your ever-virtuous champion friends!

I stopped dead in my tracks. Najib and Bijan. I hoped that whatever Polly had done to them, whatever magic she had cast to make them fall into such a deep sleep, was not permanent. My thoughts paused for a moment on Bijan. His dimpled smile and curly black hair. His blind dedication to ending all that was dark and wrong, and aiding all that was pure and good. The simplicity of his moral compass was enviable; I wish I had been able to navigate my more intimate dilemmas without drowning in a murky pool of ambivalent grey. The thought of Bijan left a sour taste in my mouth and a crinkle in my heart. I hadn't been expecting that. It had been a long time since someone made me feel like he did.

"Gerome, did you hear me?" barked Polly, snapping me back to reality.

"Uh?"

"I told you to drink from the fountain!"

Somehow, my feet had begrudgingly led me to an imposing fountain in the middle of a vast square plaza. Despite the wear and tear of a decade of demonic control, the intricate mosaic that decorated the plaza's pavement seemed, for the most part, unscathed. It appeared to depict a light being of sorts – maybe a saint or a deity dear to the locals. There was a radiant helmet atop the idol's head. This had to be an image of Agris of the Lighthelm. My gaze followed the folk hero's extended hand. It seemed to lead the viewer's eye to the foot of a sprawling set of stone steps. At the top of the stairs stood two formidable doors covered in ornate ironwork, the entrance to a building so ominous it had to be a religious structure.

"Let me guess, Lighthelm Cathedral," I grunted.

There was no doubt in my mind we'd reached our destination. The building loomed like a demanding parent over the minuscule faithful beneath it. I could practically smell its sanctimonious stink. The cathedral's foreboding walls were the dark grey of storm clouds, weathered by the touch of centuries of rain and bird droppings. Towering spires projected towards the heavens and cast long shadows over the plaza and anyone who dared approach it. Chipped statues were nestled in the alcoves along the building's impressive facade, their hands raised to the sky and their faces warped in looks of hesitant glee. Like the divine rapture had gotten a bit too real.

Polly shrugged as if she couldn't care less. "Whatever. I told you to drink!"

My gaze followed her finger. She was pointing at the grand fountain beside which we'd stopped. Or better, its contents. The ornate water feature must have fetched the artisan guild a pretty penny in its day. No expense had been spared. The main pool was broad enough to bathe an elephant. At its centre was a three-tiered set of basins, decreasing in size but increasing in grandiosity. There were fish faces with holed mouths that had run dry, lion paws carved along the marbled sides for mock support, and an excessive number of naked cherubs. The squirting water had long stopped functioning in the absence of a working pump. Now, the remaining water was stagnant and pitch black. My favourite kind of drinking water.

"Yuck. I'm telling you, Polly, something or someone died in this."

"Who knows? Don't think about it too much."

"You're serious, aren't you?"

"It's the only way to be able to enter the cathedral. My father said so."

She glanced up towards the floating corpse as if to confirm her statement. The shadow's eyeless skull moved up and down in what I assumed was a meek nod.

"Oh, is that the case? Well, I guess I'll take a big swig of it if Daddy says so!"

Polly didn't own a sense of humour. Her fists curled into balls. "Drink it, or else."

Spores started spinning in furious revolutions around us both.

"Or what?" I baited her. "You've taken me hostage. I don't know what you've done to the others but it can't be anything good. And you seem to have some ambiguous plan in mind for me and my resident demon. So, screw you, Polly."

"Uuuuuhhh," moaned Bingop-ul.

There was a tense moment of glowering. Polly's stance eased.

"I'll give you the mushroom."

"Okay then. Sure."

I am such a man-whore. My hand stretched out expectantly. Polly's eyes locked on mine before tossing the orange mushroom in my direction. Her hatred for physical contact was very much alive. I picked the mushroom off the ground, blew off a speck of dirt, and downed it without ceremony.

The effects were immediate. Al's stifling presence quickly receded into an anonymous corner of my mind. At least, for as long as it took the chemicals to dissipate from my system.

I hardly had time to savour my relief.

"Drink," growled Polly, her tone laced with threats. "No time to waste."

"Sheesh, give me a minute."

I dunked a hesitant hand in the fountain water. It was exactly the consistency I expected. Thicker than soup and runnier than cement. I cupped a shallow puddle in my palms and pretended to sip at it. Most of it dripped straight through the gaps in my fingers.

Polly was unimpressed.

"I'm not a moron, Gerome! Get on with it!"

"Okay, okay," I muttered, keenly aware of the spores nipping at my ears.

I took a tiny gulp of black water this time.

It was as terrible as I'd predicted. Like pure evil's public latrine. The most revolting thing I'd tasted since Kerwin, brother number four, had taken to making breakfast for his younger siblings, me included.

I didn't have much time to dwell on the flavour, however.

I leaned on the fountain's ledge, my stomach churning. Violent stabs of discomfort rippled through my body. The world had begun to wobble. I closed my eyes tight, supplicating any deity or supernatural being within earshot – even one as mediocre as Agris of the Lighthelm – to come to my aid.

No one did.

As I wobbled.

Out of existence.

Wobble.

Wobble.

Wobble.

Chapter Seven

THE DEMON AND THE BABY

Wobble.

Wobble.

Wobble.

As an arcane practitioner, I can confidently say that the most apt description of the phenomenon I had experienced could be captured by a five-word statement.

"That was some funky shit," I stammered through gritted teeth.

I was fearful of opening my eyes straight away. You can study magic all your life and it will still find ways to amaze you. And scare the crap out of you.

I felt a spray of cool droplets on my face. Reality appeared to have returned to a solid state.

With some degree of relief, I realised I hadn't moved. I was still stooped over the fountain, my hand dripping wet. But now the water was clear. The fountain was spouting wide arching jets into the ether. The occasional sprays would catch in the breeze and speckle my skin. I spotted a shoal of colourful fish gliding through the pool, their golden tails flashing in the light. I looked up. Sunshine. I could not believe how much I'd missed it.

This was Elderstay. The Elderstay from before the disaster. When it still resembled a family-friendly holiday destination. I leaned back and let my sickly pale complexion feel the warm touch of natural light. I would have basked in this private moment of serenity forever. Had a lot of people not bossily encroached on my range of vision.

I detected a human male draped in black robes, so long they dragged along the ground. He was slowly ascending Lighthelm Cathedral's stairs. I could tell the man's garments were finely made, the quality you'd expect to be worn by a regent or aristocrat. But, unlike most noblemen I'd met, he flaunted no trimmings or insignia. No decorations or vibrancy. Just black. The black of mourning.

It was Lord Edmund of Elderstay.

I do not know how I knew. I just did.

He was being followed by a noisy crowd of people. Men and women, most of them elderly, draped in white clothing with gold lacing, in stark contrast to their Lord. Priests and priestesses clad in the plentiful devotion of their faithful's pockets. The general effect was that of a hunched crow pursued by clucking doves.

I did not hear what they were saying. Their voices were distorted, as if I was eavesdropping through an impenetrable glass pane. No one appeared to have seen me. I was not entirely sure I could be seen.

Lord Edmund did not stop or pay them any heed. He was leaning in on himself, clutching something tight to his chest, as if afraid someone might snatch it from him. As he approached the cathedral's entrance, he turned to face the crowd. His features were stretched in the unmistakable look of grief. One all the races in the world shared.

I caught a glimpse of the bundle he'd been holding and my heart dipped an inch.

A lifeless baby.

The poor thing was dwarfed in its father's hands. Its skin almost blue.

The white-wearing crowd stopped at the foot of the stairs. Seemingly none would take a step further. I could not hear the sour remonstrations volleyed between the lone man and the ecclesiastic gathering, but I got the general gist of it. They were telling the Lord not to. *Not to what?*

Edmund turned his back on them and stepped through the open doors. He didn't care for their admonishments. To my surprise, no one pursued him. Yet their faces were etched with worry.

With a sudden lurch, I was propelled forward through space. Technically, I had remained still, but my surroundings whooshed past me as Lord Edmund disappeared from my range of vision. When I got my bearings, I found

I was now crouching behind a pillar within Lighthelm Cathedral itself. Odd, since I'd been befriending a coterie of ravenous goldfish by the fountain outside a moment before.

I watched from my shaded cover as the Lord stepped through the poorly lit nave, past the rows of vacant aisles, his feet echoing in the empty house of worship. He was headed for the altar at the far end of the hall.

There was an unholy crash as the Lord tossed something aside and laid the bundled child on the altar. The father did so with heart-breaking tenderness. Unlike how carelessly he'd hurled away the holy item that had been on the altar, placed at just the right angle to capture the rays of sun that winked through the round gap in the ceiling.

I was not one for religion but I knew this much. Every religious structure was erected around a sacred relic. Said artefacts would be positioned with great ceremony in a prominent place. Usually in well-lit conditions, using strategically placed windows to elicit a sense of awe in simpletons. The relic could be a holy toothpick for all people cared. As long as it had belonged to a god or some close approximation. As long as the showmanship was there. The feeling of existential transcendence. The make-believe.

I squinted at the object, inert in the dust. The rusted helmet Lord Edmund had so unceremoniously discarded had to be *it*. The sacred relic the cathedral had been named after. Of course. It was *in* the name. *Lighthelm.*

For people of sturdy faith, rejecting their god leaves a vacuum of sorts. One that, to the subtle disembodied energies floating about the ether, is equivalent to a flare gun blast in the night. I wondered if the man knew this. If he had intended for this to happen…

Lord Edmund began to mutter words imbued with dark purpose. Maybe a prayer. Or a chant. Yet it had none of the musical inflections of a benevolent ditty. The cathedral seemed to grow slightly colder. Perhaps even a tad dimmer.

There was a whimper. Not from me.

Had it not been for the swift recollection that my presence here was merely an illusion, I would have bolted from the cathedral in terror.

A little girl was standing next to me.

She was completely enthralled with Lord Edmund. And, unsurprisingly, very much unaware of the gnome in her vicinity. I scrutinised my new accomplice. The little girl was wearing a lace dress, tastefully embroidered with hand-stitched floral patterns. Her shoes were well made: tanned leather that had been dyed pastel with a little red ribbon on the tip. Not commoner's clothing. I had an eye for that kind of thing.

The child stood at about my height. Had she been a gnome, I would have placed her at approximately twelve or thirteen years of age. Being human, she was likely half that. She did not resemble the local scurvy-ridden and grey-faced northerners such as the ones I'd met in Snowden. Her head was crowned by a mane of frizzy black hair and she had a dark brown complexion. One common among inhabitants of the coastal regions. *Why does she look familiar?*

That's when it all went wrong.

There was a sound. One that does not belong on this side of the veil. One that conjures images that should stay where they cannot be heard, let alone seen. I turned my head to the source and wished I hadn't.

The baby on the altar. It wasn't a baby anymore.

Every arcane practitioner knows to fear demons. We have history. I understood this more intimately than most. While in their dimension, demons exist solely as unexpressed malevolent energy that sways around in the Shade Planes' billowing darkness – truly awful stuff can happen when they cross over to our side. Where once had been the tragic remains of a newborn, now was something far more sinister.

Lord Edmund stopped chanting and looked up.

The baby's body – the gelatinous consistency of foul swamps and rotting corpses – had begun to swell. The altar moaned and cracked beneath its weight. Tendrils shot from its engorging form and plunged through the cathedral's stained-glass windows. It was growing so fast it was practically scrubbing the frescoes off the ceiling.

Lord Edmund cried in horror. And did what, by all accounts, anyone with some sense would have done. He spun around and sprinted towards the exit. Had the Lord made up his mind a mere second earlier, it might have saved his life.

Edmund was almost at the doors when an enormous lumpy hand lurched through the aisles. The force of the displaced air slammed the long benches into each other. The sticky, foul appendage wrapped around the Lord's waist with a sickening squelch and dragged him back. Back towards the gaping void of bone-like teeth that was the monster's mouth.

I looked away. I wish the little girl had, too.

There was a horrifying *crunch*. A stifled gasp.

No.

"Daddy..." she sobbed.

Oh. No.

I tried. I did.

I attempted to cover the girl's ears from the damp thud, as what remained of Lord Edmund was cast off on the floor. To shield her from the debris falling from the punctures in the cathedral's ceiling. To hug her, at least. Wipe away the tears streaming unchecked down her cheeks. Lie to her, like an adult must to a child. Say things like, *it's going to be okay*, despite having no proof or belief it ever would be.

But I was just a spectator. There was nothing I could do.

I was forced to watch as the little girl hobbled, pale and shell-shocked, towards the exit and slipped through the crack in the doors.

I took a steadying breath and ran after her.

Outside, Elderstay was in chaos and the little girl nowhere to be seen. People were running about, calling for their loved ones, overturning stalls and trampling each other in an attempt to get as far from Lighthelm Cathedral as they could. The air was filled with the prayers and supplications of priestesses and priests, trying to summon their Lighthelm god. Whatever they feared might happen, had indeed happened in a spectacularly disastrous fashion. I'm pretty sure I heard one of the clergymen praise the newcome demon. Can't blame a guy for making one last-ditch attempt to save his skin.

The sizzling sound of destructive magic shook my surroundings as beams of light poured through the cracks in the cathedral's ceiling, staining the blue sky with mustardy blemishes. Soon, the evil glow blocked out the sun and moulded itself into the shape of a massive dome which encompassed the whole city, sentencing the inhabitants to a macabre half-life. The Lighthelm god was defiled. Elderstay was under new management.

The rest was history.

Wobble.

Wobble.

Wobble

"Finally!" an unpleasant voice snapped in my ear. One I was well acquainted with by now. "What took you so long?"

I woke to find myself hugging the edge of the fountain. I couldn't see my reflection this time, or anything else for that matter. I shouldn't have been surprised. The colourful goldfish had perished and decayed at the bottom of the basin years ago. The thought induced a tingling sense of absence in the pit of my stomach. I stared emptily into the filthy water. Then up, at the cloying yellow barrier above our heads. A heavy silence filled the air for what felt like a very long time. The disjointed clues were falling into place, and I thought I had it. I almost had it.

"Come on, gnome!" scolded Polly. "You were out cold for ages! You just took a tiny sip!" Her tone was tinged with urgency. I noticed her lips were stained black. Mine must have been too. "Come on, let's go inside!"

"It was the baby," I said. "The demon was the baby. Lord Edmund was trying to strike a deal with the Shade Planes. To bring his child back to life…"

I could feel Polly's gaze on me. The loyal Bingop-ul was next to her; the undead goblin seemed oddly subdued.

"But you already knew that," I continued, "didn't you, Polly?"

That's why she looked familiar. Beneath years of subtle magical alterations, I saw the face of the little girl. The one who had hidden behind a pillar and witnessed evils no child ever should. Her frizzy black hair had all but dropped out, replaced by odd lichen-like growths. The kind you expect to find on the side of damp caves or the bark of gnarly old trees. Her skin had gone from a healthy rich brown to an unnatural sandy tinge. She was like a plant that had grown in the shade. Sheltered from the light in more than one way. Everything about her had morphed, spoiled. Except for her inky black eyes. Those had remained the same. And they were currently set on me with disarming intensity.

"What are you talking about?" growled Polly, a threat in her tone.

"You are Lord Edmund's daughter."

I did not need her to confirm this. The look she gave me was enough.

I ambled past Polly, taking care to avoid her spores. I needn't have worried. Like their caster, the magical swirling spores had gone still, as if frozen in place.

I stopped and turned back, pacing up and down the plaza with my hands behind my back. One of my little habits when trying to catch up with my thoughts. I felt them stumble over each other in an unseen race towards some grand realisation. I had been known to fall into such deep states of ambling cogitation, I am told that – to this day – you can still see where my incessant walking stripped a path in my first arcane teacher's lawn. A lot was going on, there was a lot to think about. A lot to do. To find a way to stop this curse, lift it…

"How did you find out?" asked Polly, breaking my train of thought.

I stopped, knowing that, despite how much I wanted to sort out Elderstay's demon conundrum, the girl required my complete attention.

"After I drank that disgusting filth you forced me to guzzle, I wobbled out of this place and time into some simulated memory of the past. The past in which *this*," I lifted my hands to the sky, "gigantic balls-up happened."

"How did you do that? How did you see the past?" Polly looked at the fountain, almost reproachfully. "That didn't happen to me!"

"I'm a wizard." That was my standard reply when I did something cool but had no idea how exactly.

"So, you saw what happened? With my father and the helmet?" Her voice dipped to an almost inaudible whisper, "And my little brother…?"

I nodded.

There was a long pause.

"Did my dad do it on purpose? Summon a demon?"

"I don't think so. But you said it yourself: the Lighthelm was a divine artefact gifted to your ancestor, Agris, by an ancient deity. By refuting a god in their place of worship and removing said god's sacred item from the altar… It left a void to be filled. It was an act bound to attract negative attention. I don't think Lord Edmund knew what he was calling over. He may have been seeking any force or entity that could bring his child back. And, technically, the demon fulfilled its side of the deal. The baby did come back. In a manner of speaking. Demons are true to their word. You just won't like how they'll go about it."

I spotted the prime culprit in this sad story, staring at me with eyeless orbs from a few feet above my head.

"Greetings, Your Lordship." I curtsied at the floating half-man in the tattered black robes. "I guess, I can't fault your motives. 'A' for effort but it will be an 'F' for the outcome."

The hovering remains of Lord Edmund acknowledged me with a sad guttural rasp. I turned back to Polly. "I have to ask. How did your little brother, you know…?"

"He was stillborn." I watched as the girl's feet teased at the mosaic pieces on the ground, her eyes downcast, lost someplace else. "My mum died too. Complications. When we lost them both, Dad would have done anything in the world to fix what happened… He'd always wanted a boy to pass on the—" Polly stopped, her gaze lifting to meet mine. "The Lighthelm? In your vision of the past did you see where it went?"

"The helmet is probably long gone, by now." I hesitated. I didn't want to pry further. But a part of me knew I had to. "What happened to you, after Lighthelm Cathedral?"

She shrugged and wrapped her arms around herself. "It doesn't matter."

"It matters to me."

Polly seemed taken aback by this. She sat down on the ledge of the fountain. The first time she'd dropped her defences. The girl always looked like she was ready to fight or flee at any moment; she loved the things she could control completely and destroyed what she could not. Now I think I knew why.

"People were running. I ran with them. I made it out of the main gates before the dome closed off the city, but the bridge was so crowded… People were pushing and stumbling over each other. Someone shoved into me… I fell and stumbled down the ravine."

"Did no one come looking for you?"

"My parents were dead." Polly glanced at the hovering corpse of her father, before looking back at me. "There was no one left who cared about me."

"Oh."

"I was lucky, I guess. In the fall I hadn't broken any bones but I'd twisted my ankle. I found a cave and crawled inside it. I was hungry. No one could hear me. No one came for me. Until *they* did."

"Who did?"

"I cannot speak of them. They said never to speak of them. Especially not to a wizard."

That didn't wholly surprise me. "Seems fair. If that's what *they* said…"

Polly's face scrunched up in a deeply focused expression. When she looked back at me, I knew something within her had relented. "They didn't have a name. So, I called them Mushy. They wouldn't speak to me, not at first. Yet they would grow around me when I was cold. Feed me when I was hungry. Mushy took care of me. Until they became a part of me."

A spark went off in my brain. The spores.

"A Leshi!" I gasped.

"A what?"

The common folk knew them by the name of "forest guardians" or "tree spirits". That was derivative and imprecise. Leshi didn't just have a soft spot for trees. In magical circles, they were regarded as entities that dwelled somewhere between solid and gaseous states. At times, they would become devoted – for poorly understood reasons – to a stone, cave, or brook. They proceeded to care for such natural features and would defend them with their lives. Ultimately, they would take on the aspect of what they cared for. Leshi were very much unstudied, mainly because they would never show themselves to the likes of arcane researchers. Nor would they allow themselves to be sampled, prodded, and inspected for analysis, which was a bummer for esoteric naturalists. Yet I could not blame the Leshi. That explained the creature's hesitancy in revealing itself to me. Wizards had a history of unkindness towards *other* kinds of magical wielders. If it didn't have two hands, two legs, and a head, we hardly believed it to be a sentient spellcaster at all.

"I can explain later." I paused. "… I am sorry for what happened to you, Polly. What you witnessed in Lighthelm Cathedral as a child. The destruction of Elderstay. Your family… No one should have to endure that."

Polly's eyebrows converged on her forehead, her nails digging fiercely into her palms. "All this happened because of that blasted helmet, you know?"

"What does the Lighthelm have to do with it?" I asked confused.

"It has everything to do with it! The Lighthelm has caused my family nothing but problems! Some stupid tradition says the helmet can only ever be passed down to the first male heir, to keep the god's gift pure or something like that. My uncle, Lord Brent, was the second born, and he was always jealous of my father for being the keeper of the Lighthelm. And the reason my father was so desperate for a boy was so he could pass the helmet on to a successor. With a girl, the Agris bloodline would be broken." Polly took a staggered breath. "I wasn't enough."

I could tell how much this pained her. I remembered how baffled I had been after relocating to Grandfall. It was not the food, the greetings, and how people hung their laundry that took getting used to. Humans had a *gender* thing. My understanding was that titles and inheritances went to boys, irrespective of age or reasoning abilities. It was common for girls from wealthy families to be married off young or ordained in some religious order as priestesses and nuns. The ones from poorer backgrounds worked as hard as their male counterparts, often for little to no reward. The system hadn't sat well with my gnomish sensibilities. In Underdwell, we live in a high-functioning anarchy where women make up less than one-tenth of the population. Girls, born far more seldom than boys, are regarded as a treasured gift. My mother would have happily traded one of us for a girl. Maybe even thrown in a few more to sweeten the deal.

I sensed how vulnerable Polly felt. Since our journey began, she had known my weaknesses. Used them even. Now I did hers. I knew her story and her worst nightmares. She was like a stunned bird that had flown into a shut window. Her heart was in the palms of my hands. And I wasn't about to squeeze the life out of her. I knew a thing or two about sorrow.

"Polly…"

I stopped dead.

An amplified crashing sound tugged at my senses. Like a charging rhinoceros wearing steel boots. I turned just in time to see a gigantic armoured man, storming towards me at full speed.

"I smite evil!" he bellowed with a voice like the screech of metal on metal.

Najib swung his sword. Had I been human, my head would have been at the bottom of the fountain by now. Being as tall as your average dustbin does have its advantages. I ducked for cover and scarpered as far from the champion as I could.

To his credit, Bingop-ul did try to help. The undead goblin staggered towards Najib, his fists raised for a fight. And was promptly cleaved in two.

"No!" cried Polly.

Before I had time to register what had happened, the floating remains of Lord Edmund wrapped around Najib like a cantankerous blanket. The shadowy corpse of His Lordship was trying to protect his daughter. One last heroic attempt to make up for the daddy issues, I guess.

With the sickening sound of cracking bones and tearing cloth, Lord Edmund was sliced down by the murderous colossus. Najib was like I had never seen him. His usual sluggish movements and quiet demeanour had always conjured an almost *bovine* image in my mind. Perhaps that of a mellow castrated steer who spent his days asexually ruminating in a paddock. My kindly picture of Najib was quickly being superimposed by that of an impregnable maniac, brandishing a massive sword. He moved with deadly efficiency. Once he had finished hacking poor Lord Edmund to even smaller bits, the dark gaps in his helmet turned to Polly.

"Najib!" I screamed. "Stop! Don't hurt her!"

He didn't listen. Najib started towards the girl.

Polly's eyes widened in panic. The spores shot from her hands, striking at the grooves in his helmet, seeking the gaps in his armour plates. They had no effect. Najib kept coming. Nothing could halt his approach, the relentless clang of his boots like the sounding of an execution drum. He loomed over her. I watched as the sword lifted above his head, a stroke away from ending her life.

I had done my fair share of watching bad things happen. I couldn't – I *wouldn't* – do that again.

I like to tell myself it was Al who made me do it. After all, this is my recollection of events. I am allowed to remember the past as I please. So, it was Al's fault. End of story.

The fireball erupted from me with the force of a thousand suns.

The blast ricocheted through the air, propelling itself with earth-shattering power towards Najib. The flames engulfed the man. All I could see was the black outline of his armour, until that too vanished from sight in the red hellscape. The fireball didn't stop. It blew a moon-sized hole in the building directly behind where Najib had been.

Of Bijan's brother, the faithful champion of Radia and prince of Sipera, there was nothing but a smouldering pile of molten metal and bits of silver strewn across the mosaic tiles on the ground.

I have some vague notion that I dropped to my knees, my hand still outstretched and smoking. The taste of bile coating my mouth, the smell of burning filling my nostrils as half the apartment block collapsed in on itself in a fiery heap of rubble. I felt someone tug me gently. I vaguely registered that Polly's hand was wrapped around my shoulder.

"Gerome, we have to go…"

I heard running. Heavy boots against stone. A scream of anguish.

"Please, Gerome…"

I allowed her to help me up.

We somehow reached the stairs to the cathedral. Then we moved through a small gap between its doors. There was a magical screech. Not unlike the sound the dome enveloping the city had made when my spellcasters attacked it with their life-destroying hex. There had been another arcane barrier protecting the entrance to the cathedral. The black water Polly had forced me to drink had done its job. I couldn't bring myself to ask why or how.

I glanced back over my shoulder before we vanished behind the doors.

Bijan. He was staring straight at me, as he kneeled beside whatever was left of Najib. Sha-sha was next to him, impassive. I saw the look in his eyes. I knew what it meant. Bijan would have his revenge.

As I allowed Polly to coax me into the darkness, I wondered.

What side have I chosen?

Chapter Eight

THE BLOOD OF DARKNESS

Our staggering footsteps echoed through the silent cathedral. Followed, shortly afterwards, by a loud crash as we stumbled over jagged shapes in the dark.

"Fuck," snarled Polly, getting up. A plume of spores rose off her as she patted herself down. "This place is a mess!"

She extended a hand to help me up. I didn't take it.

I lugged myself into a sitting position on the cold stone floor. My shoulders found something solid – an overturned bench. It was uncomfortable but it would do, for now.

I stared vacantly at my surroundings. The sense of déjà vu was uncanny. In the pockets of yellow light oozing from the punctured ceiling, Lighthelm Cathedral was much as I remembered it. Just grimier. Sparse pieces of rubble piled up along the cracked flooring. Several fractures had stretched up the supporting pillars that lined the nave. The long benches, once host

145

to countless faithful rears, had been mostly tossed about and splintered. *The rusty old helmet and namesake of the cathedral, might still be here somewhere.* Kicked to some secluded corner of the hall or flattened to a pancake by a fallen column. Everything was as the demon-baby had left it more than a decade earlier. As far as I could ascertain from my current position, the cathedral was currently devoid of the slimy monstrosity nightmares are made of. Though I couldn't help but notice the rather conspicuous crater in the floor where the altar had been. Now, if I was a betting man…

I could feel Polly's eyes on me in the gloom. She was fidgeting on the spot. I doubted her stunted social skills extended to knowing how to deal with someone in emotional turmoil. I was in no mood to go over the basics. At last, she left me to it. I could hear her searching the cathedral for something, lifting fallen chattels and kicking about debris. After staring into mid-space for some time, I got to my feet and stumbled off to a candle alcove in the wall. My boots felt like they were made of lead. As soon as I reached the alcove, I pressed my hands against the cold marble. The next minute, I was doubled over, throwing up whatever little I had in my stomach. The taste of the black water tainted my mouth. A pulsating sensation was shooting through my palm, still hot from the blast. A dull feeling in my head, as if someone had hit me from behind with a chair and knocked my soul clean out of my body.

I'd taken a life. I'd *killed* Najib.

"Gerome," started Polly. I could feel her gaze on the back of my head. "We can't stay here."

I made a non-committal sound.

"They'll figure it out sooner or later. How to get inside the cathedral. The purpose of the fountain water… Bijan's not smart enough but the snake woman is. Sha-sha," she added as if I'd have trouble recalling who best fit that description.

"Yes, Sha-sha. She's terrifying, isn't she?" I chuckled mirthlessly.

"I liked her. More than the…" Polly thought better than to finish that sentence. "Thank you. You know, for saving my life."

"Please. Don't."

I wiped my mouth and returned to my spot against the overturned bench with no plans of getting back up any time soon.

Polly sighed audibly. "Okay, five more minutes."

She joined me on the floor, positioning herself much closer than I had expected her to, though I couldn't have cared less about breathing in a lungful of toxic spores right then. I couldn't help noticing that Polly's demeanour towards me had changed for the better. I guess some friendships can be kindled in the warm glow of blazing murder.

"Why are we here, Polly?" A drop of venom had trickled into my tone. "If we were going to Lighthelm

Cathedral anyway, why not go with the others? All together? In the morning? As we'd planned!"

I admit it, I was angry. And sad. And keen to share the landslide of guilt tumbling down on my narrow shoulders.

"They wouldn't have understood. I needed you. And your demon."

"I'm not some *tool* for you to whip out and use at a whim, Polly! I'm a person! Najib was a person! And now, because of us, Najib is dead! His beloved brother will be out for our blood and rightly so! As for Sha-sha, I'm betting she'll be wondering which wine pairs best with gnome. If it was Brent's precious reward you were after—"

"You know it was not," she mumbled. The finality in her tone drained the fight from me.

"Why do you think Najib attacked us?" she asked after a moment.

I gave a brooding shrug. "I guess we must have looked like we were up to something bad. Picture it. You and me after dark, strolling about the city in the company of two undead. Then we proceeded to drink filth from some cursed fountain. Like that's a normal activity at two o'clock in the morning. Najib must have thought we were cavorting with the enemy. With all due respect, Polly, you don't exactly have a pristine track record with what happened with Bingop-ul. And I'm... I'm compromised."

"Najib could have asked us. He just went ahead and…" Polly swallowed whatever sorrow she had left to feel. I wondered what it was like; to mourn people who had not been alive in the conventional meaning of the word.

She was right about one thing, though. Najib could have attempted some small degree of diplomacy. Instead, he had come tearing into us like a bull on steroids. There had been no stopping him. I had to tell myself that. I had to.

"So," I asked, keen to change the subject, "how did you find out about my, erm, demon problem? It's not something I advertise in big print on the back of my robes: *demon overlord on board*."

"I didn't know at first. Hell, I never even thought I'd set foot in Elderstay again after what happened. Mushy and I spent years travelling the roads, going wherever took our fancy. I had no plans of ever returning home – not until I heard of my Uncle Brent's quest to retake Elderstay. It was my dad's city – *my* city. So, I put my hand up to join. They didn't ask many questions. All that interested Brent was that I could do what I said I could." Spores danced about her head as she spoke, swaying to the sound of her voice.

"Did Brent not recognise his own niece?" I was astounded. I had my fair share of nieces and nephews, all of whom I cherished. I remembered every name, every birthday. It pained me terribly to think I'd probably gained a few more since my last visit. I hadn't returned to Underdwell in a couple of years. I wasn't comfortable going to see my relatives, burdened as I was with a world-ending demon.

"No. You saw him in the Grand Hall. He's an ass. Brent didn't even notice when I told him my name…" Polly sneered at the thought of her self-interested uncle.

"You still haven't explained how you knew about my demon."

"I'm getting there. Do you remember when we found the blood circle? That was the first time I heard my dad's voice."

"Your dad's voice?" I thought back with some reticence to the awful gory scene. Polly had stepped through the blood circle after Najib. "Is that why you crossed over, even when it was clearly a terrible idea?"

She nodded uneasily. "My dad told me to. After the blood circle, he kept talking to me. He would speak in whispers and riddles, sometimes so quietly I could barely understand him. His voice became louder as we got closer to Elderstay. The stuff he said didn't always make sense, but there was one thing he kept saying over and over. That there was an evil spellcaster in our group. One who carried a dark presence within them. One so powerful, it could stop my little brother and lift the curse." Polly studied me in a way I didn't quite know how to interpret. "I thought it was Sha-sha at first. Then, I realised it was you."

My mouth opened and closed without making sensible noises. "Is that why you needed me – *us* – here?!"

"My little brother is a demon. I need your demon to defeat him."

Demon trumps demon. In theory, it's true. In practice, it's batshit crazy.

"Oh, well," I shook my head, clasping my hands together in a melodramatic gesture. "Had you told me that sooner, I would have informed you that the answer is – and, make no mistake, it always will be – *no can do*."

Polly folded her arms, spores wafting angrily around us both. "Why?"

"Because that would mean letting said demon take over my body." I laughed, in a slightly manic fashion. "You think what I did back there was destructive? Imagine what might happen if you leave a talented wizard in the hands of a demon who has no qualms about hurting anyone or anything! Demons are like live-wired cables to a spellcaster's magic. With me as his puppet, my demonic fiend would be strong enough to fireball the whole planet to oblivion! And he'd probably love that idea. Also, for your information, despite what your father may have told you, I'm not an *evil* wizard. I've just made some questionable life choices."

"Isn't it an evil wizard thing, to have a demon?" asked Polly, insistently. "Didn't you, like, summon it?"

Touché. It was an *evil* wizard thing. And, yes – strictly speaking – I would have had to summon it. Demons hadn't always been lounging around the Shade Planes waiting for a rip in the cosmological tapestry. We had all been happily unaware of each other. Until some hapless arcane practitioner, some untold number of millennia ago, had unstitched the seams between dimensions, and the very first demon had made the crossing. The wand-waving idiot was duly possessed and went rogue. She or he became the first "Evil Witch" or "Evil Wizard", depending on who tells the story – the wizards or the witches. As for the story's details, at least the ones we can all agree on: spellcasters rallied from all over. Wanting to clear our name, and avoid the chop from the higher authorities, the best magical minds of the time united in what later became known as the Enchanted Institution. The "Evil Witch-slash-Wizard" was defeated.

But the demon must have slithered back to the Shade Planes and told the others it had a lot of fun. After that first breach, demons became obsessed with us, and the Enchanted Institution is all that stands between the chaos of their world and the order of ours. And it takes its job very seriously. Those practitioners who toyed with the veil between our world and the Shade Planes met inventively painful and devilishly architected punishments that would make even the most badass magical renegades beg for the sweet release of death.

"I didn't mean to summon it," I murmured at last. "It just kind of happened."

"So, if you're not evil, how did you get to have a demon?"

There it was. The question. The one I hoped no one would ever ask. And that I would never have to answer. I almost missed the version of Polly who hardly spoke at all.

"It doesn't matter."

"It matters to me."

"I see what you did there." I snickered. "Let's say, I cared about someone a lot. I wanted them to care about me too. I did something stupid. A demon got mixed up in it. It's messy."

"Perhaps you can tell me later. After we deal with my brother."

"If we go down there," I nodded at the chasm at the end of the hall, "there isn't going to be a *later*, Polly…"

"Gerome," she began, "I am going to stop my brother with or without you. I'd much rather it be with you. And your demon." She got up. "But, if you'd like to sit here until Bijan and Sha-sha arrive, that's fine by me."

Polly looked at the doors and then back at me. No sign of either of them, for now. Sha-sha was not as smart as Polly had assumed. Or the snake woman was too busy eating Bijan. That horrid thought made me cold to the marrow.

Without another word, Polly started to make her way towards the chasm.

"Okay," I said, actually feeling my better judgement shake its head at me. "I will come with you, *but*," and I lifted my index finger in admonishment, "I am not letting Al out."

I felt so much like my mother.

"Al?" Polly smirked. "You gave your demon a name?"

"After my first ex. Horrible piece of work."

"Was she called Alice or something?"

His name was Altair. But we'd done enough sharing for one day.

I reached inside my boot. "There is one last thing I need to do before we go."

"What?"

"Write a quick letter."

"To who?"

"To *whom* it may concern."

"Concerning what?"

"The end of the world. In case I die, and Al gets out. Or I become his slave, and Al gets out. Or the demons join forces, and Al gets out. I don't know, Polly, I'm spitballing here." I could tell she didn't get it. "I just need someone, *anyone*, to know."

"Know what?"

"That I'm sorry."

Polly assessed me. It was rather clear she thought I was a moron, but she had the delicacy not to inform me out loud.

"Okay," she conceded, "but you have *one* minute."

I pulled out the blank pieces of parchment, courtesy of Bellamy Kirt. Despite my earlier promise to myself, it seemed more and more likely I'd be joining the scout soon, after all. On that note…

To whom it may concern,

If you are reading this, I am indubitably dead. That's a good word to add a touch of whimsy to one's epitaph. Here lies the indubitably dead so-and-so. Please know, dear reader, I did not want to die. I very much liked living. As everyone could attest to at my local, the Roaring Peacock. Since you are looking at my disfigured and indubitably dead remains, let me tell you my name was Gerome.

Gerome the gnome.

Yes, I get that a lot.

This, dear reader, is my story as told by me. A version much unlike the one you may gather from campfire tales, read in books, or hear from your grandma in the years to come. If there are to be campfires, books, grandmas, or years to come, for that matter. This is the story of how I, Gerome, magna cum laude star pupil and, later, junior lecturer at the Arcane Polytechnic in Grandfall – a dashingly handsome and promising young man – doomed the world to the unspeakable horrors of the New Dark. I understand this will mean a big fat deal to you, as you contemplate the world's final days, and all of existence being swallowed into the spiralling darkness of the Shade Planes. But, please, I must tell someone, anyone.

My bad. I am sorry.

As for why this happened, it began how all terrible things begin.

For a whiff of happiness.

And for want of hanky-panky...

I scribbled away at a few more pages, as best I could for someone using his own thighs as a writing desk, and folded my last missive in my breast pocket, next to my heart. That's usually where people kept their money, and that's the first place anyone was likely to search a body. Such is the world we live in.

"What took you so long?" asked Polly, when I finally joined her at the ledge of the abyss. "Were you writing your life story or something?"

The descent into the chasm was sticky. The foundations – which I assumed had once been made of stone, sand, and standard mortar mix – felt viscous on touch. A disgusting snot-like substance that evoked the image of crawling through a giant elephant's nostril. Or it would have, had the stuff not emitted a somewhat livery gleam, not unlike the barrier that encased Elderstay.

We moved with silent caution through the dim and unnatural light. The void in the ground appeared to be the result of something massive burrowing its oversized body through unforgiving terrain. The entry angle was steep. It wasn't as if there were many stable ledges or footholds. More than once, I lost my balance – just to feel Polly grab my coat and steady me. I can't remember when I agreed to go first. But here I was. Stumbling at the front of the line like this was all *my* idea.

The journey down was so long, I began to wonder whether we would poke out the other end of the planet. A quaint swampy continent by the name of Hopper-Tikker, the realm of the orcish clans and home to a fine tradition of smoked eel and meat curing, boasting the vastest selection of wild boar salami in the world. And a blossoming lesser-known sushi industry. I had promised myself I'd go visit Hopper-Tikker someday, in the time before Al. I'd been told the only real downside, aside from the ever-changing and humid weather, was the propensity of the locals to roast tourists on spits.

"I think we're almost there," Polly whispered in my ear, distracting me from my sudden longing for foreign cuisine.

I didn't like it. She sounded afraid. I had seldom known her to be afraid before.

"Stay close," I said, in what I hoped was a reassuring tone. "We'll figure something out."

"We should probably come up with a plan before we find the demon."

"Right," I breathed. "A plan. Got one of those?"

"Not really."

An awkward moment of silence followed.

I watched as Polly's forehead furrowed. "The demon was huge and that'll make it an easy target. We should strike. Not give it the time to react."

"You mean we should attack it? Straight away? No questions asked?"

"Have any better ideas, Gerome?"

"Fine," I conceded. "I'll fireball it in the face. That should make a dent."

"I'll use Mushy. Swarm it with toxic spores. The demon won't know what hit it."

While it was the most unoriginal plan I'd heard since Partridge added fish to the *Roaring Peacock's* Friday menu, I couldn't fault it. Nothing wrong with sticking to our strengths and taking advantage of the element of surprise.

Suddenly, I felt my boot sink up to my ankle in a puddle of ooze. We'd hit the ground floor.

Leaning forward, I peered discreetly through the opening. The underground passage had led us straight into a massive cavity. I wagered the hollow was as expansive as Lighthelm Cathedral itself, some uncertain number of feet above our heads. The mustardy light from the gelatinous discharge that lined the walls was more intense here. As my eyes gathered more details as to our surroundings, I realised it was an almost eerie replica of the wide hall we'd come from. Same rectangular layout. High ceilings. Mounds of rubbish and debris that vaguely resembled pillars. A garish version of a place of worship. As if a huge snotty child with a sand shovel had attempted the task, rather than a squad of professional builders. There was even a makeshift pile of goo where the altar was meant to be.

"Well, I never…"

"The Lighthelm," murmured Polly, her voice heavy with unspoken resentment as she glared ahead.

And they say the gods are dead. Atop the gross mound of demon mucus sat the sacred item once dear to Elderstay's inhabitants. The rusty old helmet looked much the same as when I'd last seen it – rusted and old. It had been positioned in a prime spot on the "altar", glinting ever so slightly in the malevolent light. I am no expert in demon psychology but, after living with one for a while, I think I understood.

"It's having a laugh," I whispered under my breath.

I readied myself, a nugget of incandescent heat building at the centre of my left palm. Cold sweat started dripping down my back. A sudden flash on the inside of my eyelids. Najib's outline cast against the flame. The acrid smell of smoke in my nostrils. The way his body vanished in the blaze, vaporised by my fireball. Now was not a good time. Not a good time at all to have second thoughts or guilt-ridden flashbacks.

There was a sudden surge in flavour on the tip of my tongue. *Strawberries*.

A cavernous rumbling sound came from the depths of the earth beneath us. The adrenaline yanked me back to our current predicament. I glanced at Polly. She was in full fighting mode. Her spores were circling her body, drawing sharp, aggressive circles around her outstretched arms. The girl's hands were so thick with the stuff I couldn't make out her fingers.

My heart hammering against my chest, I watched as a sequence of slender, thread-like appendages uncoiled from behind the false altar. Like gooey octopus tentacles, they fastened against the ceiling, hardening on touch with the stone and dirt. The tendrils tensed and stretched under some extraordinary strain. The demon's giant form began to appear like a horrific dawning sun. Gelatinous and misshapen, but still vaguely humanoid – in that it had a head, a bulk, and ten appendages poking from various parts of its body – the monster rose into view. Its semi-transparent, blobby form was engorged with pieces of rubble, muck, bones, and assorted unspeakableness. If there had been any doubt in my mind as to its true nature, it was put to rest.

This wasn't an innocent baby.

It was a demon.

Chapter Nine

REVOLTING REUNIONS

The monstrous creature was much larger than I remembered it. Thankfully, I was almost certain it hadn't seen us. It didn't exactly have what I would have called "eyes". Or, truth be told, it had one in the middle of its head, round and milky. The other had slid halfway down its grotesque cheek as if the whole socket had migrated past its nose. I didn't want to have to look at it more than necessary, so I'll cut off the descriptions right there.

I gave Polly the signal. The one I had made up, just then. One which I assumed she'd understand. Wrongly. Nothing happened.

"Polly, are you ready to attack…?" I hissed.

"I WAS EXPECTING YOU."

I froze to the spot, numb with fear. The voice hadn't come from the monster's direction.

"NO NEED TO LINGER ON MY DOORSTEP."

It was Polly. Speaking. In the kind of voice that would make young children wet the bed until they're grey and balding.

"PLEASE, DO COME IN..."

As if an invisible hand had pushed her from behind, Polly lost balance and fell forward. I grabbed her to break the fall – I had intended to support her smoothly on the way down, but I pretty much acted as a gnome cushion.

"What… what happened?" she breathed, as I crawled out from under her. Her chest was heaving so rapidly, I thought she might be having a heart attack.

"I don't know."

Man, I hated that sentence. But it was true. I had no idea what was going on. I dared a glimpse in the monster's direction. It was staring at us through its cloudy and displaced eyes. I contemplated our options. As I saw it, there were only three.

We could run back up the slippery hollow. Crawl, more like. While gigantic oozing tendrils came ploughing after us. And surely, we'd end up much like Lord Edmund after he'd tried to flee for his life.

We could fight. Okay, maybe *I* could fight. Polly looked like she needed to lie down with a damp cloth on her forehead in low light for the foreseeable future.

We could surrender. There were a lot of unknowns to this one. None of them were pleasant. You don't negotiate with demons. I knew this better than most.

I felt the nugget of fire reignite in my palm.

Here goes nothing.

Without warning, I was forcefully shoved to one side. Not *me*, as in my body. Me, as in Gerome. Me as in *me*. The part that defines identity. The part without which we are little more than a pretty assortment of molecular bonds and base elements. I could do nothing but watch – I had seemingly retained that ability – as some outer force moved my arm against my will. My hand extended to the fallen Polly.

"SISTER, SO GOOD TO SEE YOU. AFTER ALL THIS TIME."

As those words left my lips, the expression on Polly's face was worth a portrait. She was terrified. A part of me liked that. I wasn't sure which part. Where I stopped and the presence began.

"What are you doing to Gerome?" she snarled, scrambling to her feet, her spores whooshing around me like a hive of angry hornets.

"YOU DRANK MY BLOOD. NOW YOU AND THE TINY WIZARD BELONG TO ME."

Ah, that little chestnut.

So, this is what was happening. The tainted fountain water was demon flavoured. Polly had believed we had to drink it to be able to enter Lighthelm Cathedral. I should have realised there would likely be a price to pay. We'd unwittingly agreed to personal enslavement for the right to cross the threshold to the demon's lair. While little consolation in my current predicament, I reminded myself that drinking a random substance out of a fountain wasn't the worst thing I'd done for drugs.

"No!" cried Polly, shaking her head as if to shrug off my words. "Father would have told me! He would have told me what the water would do!"

"IT WAS NOT FATHER'S VOICE YOU HEARD IN THE CIRCLE OF BLOOD. NOR WAS IT FATHER IN THE ICE PASSAGE, WHISPERING FOR YOU TO JOIN HIM. IT WAS NOT FATHER WHO PLAYED THE PIANO WITH YOU. IT WAS NOT FATHER WHO GUIDED YOU HERE. IT WAS NOT FATHER WHO TOLD YOU TO DRINK FROM THE FOUNTAIN. IT WAS I..."

"But... Father..."

Our faces were so close, I could see the tears prick at the sides of Polly's eyes. Whatever was left of my consciousness felt her discomfort. She'd been tricked. We all had. I felt an evil ripple through my disembodied form and my lips parted again.

"... I WHO MASTER YOU ALL."

"No!" Polly shook her head again, unwilling to accept what was happening. "I came to destroy you. Gerome did, too! And we will!"

"YOU ARE ALL HERE BECAUSE I WANTED YOU HERE. EVERYTHING WENT ACCORDING TO PLAN. ALL ALONG. FROM THE FORBIDDEN HEX UNCLE BRENT WAS GIVEN TO DESTROY MY BARRIER, TO THE ATTACKS ON THE HUMANS AND GOBLINS OF SNOWDEN THAT STARTED SHORTLY AFTER. HOW UNCLE LISTENED TO THE COUNSEL OF A TRUSTED ADVISOR TO SEEK OUT PEOPLE OF TALENT. BRENT BE-LIEVED HE WAS RECRUITING THOSE MOST QUALIFIED TO EXTERMINATE A DEMON FROM ELDERSTAY. WHAT HE DID NOT KNOW WAS THAT YOU WERE ALL BEING RECRUITED BY ME."

"How?" stammered Polly. "You couldn't have done this all by yourself! Sitting here in a pile of goo at the bottom of Lighthelm Cathedral – for over a decade!" she added, her voice breaking into a whimper.

"I HAD AN ALLY ON THE OTHER SIDE. SHE GAINED UNCLE BRENT'S TRUST AND HAS PROVEN TO BE MOST USEFUL TO ME."

Polly said the words I couldn't. "Sha-sha…"

Had I been able to speak my mind, I would have cried out, "Called it!"

The snake woman is evil. How original. I mean, this wasn't breaking news for me. I hadn't liked Sha-sha from the beginning.

This revelation seemed to upset Polly, though. There were deep lines etched in her face and she appeared nauseous. More than the fact that Sha-sha was a devious reptile who had been pursuing her own mysterious and wily interests, I think Polly resented being fooled. Bijan had said something about Sha-sha being an *old friend* of his father, the sultan of Sipera. I had to wonder how far back the deception went as far as my companions – and even Brent – were concerned. I cast my mind back to my own murky recruitment process. It was most uninformative. I had been happily zonked out of my brain. But now I knew for certain: Sha-sha had sat opposite me at the *Roaring Peacock* that night, in the grey fog of my memories. If I ever got my body back, she'd be grilled snake kebab.

"Why did you want us here?" I heard Polly ask in a feeble voice.

It was strange to feel my mouth open to reply without knowing what may come out of it.

"I HAVE DRAINED THIS PLACE OF ALL ITS ENERGY. IT HAS NOTHING MORE TO OFFER ME. I WISH TO BE LIBERATED. TO BE FREED FROM ELDERSTAY. I HAVE MY SIGHTS ON GREATER THINGS..."

Let me guess.

"... THE WORLD."

Bingo. Classic demon move.

"AND NOW I HAVE MY VERY OWN PEOPLE OF TALENT, TO DO SO."

Wait, what did it say...?!

A long tendril snaked around my neck like a hangman's noose. Then, I felt something grab my arms and legs. As if by some magic, my body was snapped upwards. I watched as the same happened to Polly. We were lifted off the ground, a coiling, slimy tentacle for each limb. Spreadeagled in mid-air – in a fashion I did not find quite as enjoyable as I had the last time this had happened to me, in a more candlelit setting.

Here I hung, wondering from inside a body that was no longer my own, a most pertinent question:

Now what?

That's when I heard a metallic sound, tumbling through the opening to the underground den.

The arrival of our rescue party was announced by a sad *splat*.

Bijan landed in muck face first, armour and all. I suspected he must have tripped halfway down the slippery passage from the hall above. He'd seemingly spent the other half of the descent rolling inside his suit of armour, like a kitten in a laundry basket, until he'd hit the bottom.

Bijan's shiny breastplate was every colour but silver, and chunks of scum had dribbled in between his pauldrons and various other joints where the metal pieces fitted together. His dark curls were matted, and I noticed his leather satchel – filled with the apothecary's wares he'd dutifully purchased prior to leaving Snowden – was bubbling on the ground, sinking in a puddle of ooze. As was his full-face helmet. He tried to yank it out of the filth. Failing miserably, Bijan hauled himself into an upright stance and took in his surroundings.

I've got to hand it to him. If Bijan thought it at all peculiar to find his former companions hanging from the ceiling in a goo-drenched cave, sprawled in mid-air, and lips curled in the demon's manic smile, he didn't show it.

After a cursory glance at the two of us – his eyes lingering on me for an uncomfortable moment – Bijan's gaze homed in on the monster. Our loathsome demonic master filled much of the back end of the cavity. Bijan hesitated. I couldn't blame him. The demon was huge.

Hand clasped tight around the grimy hilt of his greatsword, Bijan trudged through the snot, sinking slightly as he went. I couldn't see him in any great detail from my position and in such dimly lit surroundings. But the thought of the brave champion gave me tingles all over. The last ray of resplendence in a world of demons, demon-sympathisers, or poor saps who just got caught up in demon drama. It was nice to know there were people in the world like Bijan to make up for the people like yours truly and company.

Sha-sha, too, had appeared from the opening, lagging a short way behind Bijan. She was moving with ease through the goo, as if in her element. What I would have given for a third hand and a clear shot.

"Demon, behold me," declared Bijan, pointing his sword in the demon's general direction. "I, servant of the light and the mighty Radia, Goddess of All-goodness, have come to s-smite thee."

Something was wrong. Not just the introduction. That was all wrong, of course. How old school to walk in on some ungodly fiend and loudly announce your presence. That particular custom was the leading cause of death among quintessential heroes. Aside from incineration by dragon, that is. As far as I was aware, most champion guilds had abandoned the traditional hero's proclamation. Now, most of them simply muttered their intentions under their breaths, as a prelude to entering dark caves, haunted castles, and eerie underground lairs. Then proceeded to slay whatever was inside in a discreet and sensible manner. But no, something was wrong *with* Bijan. He was shaking so hard I thought he'd drop his weapon.

Is he... afraid?

Before I could even begin filing that mental note, the forceful presence shoved me aside and took ownership of my tongue.

"IS THIS ONE BIJAN OR NAJIB?" I heard myself ask.

"Bijan," Sha-sha hissed obligingly.

Bijan looked in confusion from the demon to me, and then swerved around to face the snake woman. "Sha-sha, you know this – this *demon*?"

"PITY. HE IS NOT THE ONE I WANTED."

The demon had used Polly to speak for it this time. I speculated the gelatinous monster liked mixing it up for dramatic effect. Demons love playing with their food before tearing away at their unfortunate victims one morsel at a time.

Bijan's mouth dropped open. "W-what is that supposed to mean?" he stuttered.

"IT MEANS, LITTLE CHAMPION, THAT THERE IS NOTHING SPECIAL ABOUT YOU. YOU ARE OF NO USE TO ME. AND THAT IS VERY BAD NEWS. FOR YOU…"

An expression of utmost misery flashed briefly over Bijan's face. "Now wait just a minute—"

There was a visceral, gut-wrenching sound.

Bijan turned on the spot, his sword almost dropping from his gauntleted hand. Sha-sha had turned into a shape that most befitted her slippery nature. That of a giant snake with a head as large as a suitcase and a body as long as a travelling circus. Her V-shaped pupils steadied on Bijan, unblinking. Had Sha-sha been eyeing me that way, I would have relocated to any plane of existence she wasn't currently in.

"FEAST ON THE HUMAN'S FLESH."

The snake's lips parted to reveal a row of sharp hooked fangs. Poor Bijan looked around for help. With a pang in my chest, I realised it had been an automatic response. Najib had always had his back. Now Bijan was outnumbered, outwitted, and, all in all, in over his head.

I wanted to tear my eyes away from the inevitable. But the demon had made no allowances for us to blink at will. So, I watched as Bijan hopelessly swung his sword at the reptile, before it came lunging at him, teeth bared. He was propelled through the air and landed on his back where he fell flat, pinned down by the weight of his own armour. His sword had been flung out his hand and vanished in the goo.

Clunk.

There was a sickening sound. It reminded me of the time Godwin, brother number nine, had climbed a tree then fallen off and dislocated his shoulder, after an unhealthy episode of sibling peer pressure.

Sha-sha had unhinged her jaw.

I fought against the demon's presence with every ounce of will I could muster. I really did. With the same effectiveness as a child screaming at the sky to stop raining because he wants to play outside. The demon paid me no heed. It was enjoying itself. I sensed its half-formed intentions as they floated to the surface from a nebulous haze of evil purpose. It was going to make us watch Sha-sha devour Bijan. Then it was going to use us. Use us to leave Elderstay and end the world.

I wondered how history might remember me. Whatever short history might be left between then and doomsday, I mean. I liked to think I wasn't the bad guy in this story. But I wasn't the good guy, either. After all, I had set fire to one of the good guys. Another good guy was about to be gobbled up by a traitorous serpent. And I was hanging ten feet in the air, unable to move a muscle.

No.

I was going to be struck off the roll of arcane practitioners. They were going to censor my academic papers. All my years of magical research – *puff*. Gone. They might even add my name to the Enchanted Institution's blacklist. Dare I say it, I was going to be remembered as an *evil* wizard. I hoped word never got back to my family about this. Mother had invested ever so much in my education. My brothers would never have let me hear the end of it.

I sensed something tug at the edge of my homeless consciousness. Something other than the heavy demonic essence that bound my body. A voice with which I was well acquainted. One I had never been particularly happy to hear.

Until now.

Hey, little man, what did I miss?

I cannot say I was privy to what happened next. After all, I was not invited to the meeting. This, I am given to understand, took place on some other plane of existence altogether. One which ill-befits the mind of a small humanoid mortal, as it was put to me. One in which shapes and sizes, colour and sound, up and down, and the universal laws that hold together the cosmos that we casually define as "real life", hold no meaning. In essence, I was told to stand in a corner and shut my trap because it was all a bit much for my limited gnomish intellect. In this plane of existence, there are just two forces. The darkness. And the evil that dwells within it.

If, indeed, there was something worth seeing, I suspect it'd be nothing but an endless expanse of black silt or sand, constantly being torn apart and reshaped by a wicked and equally black gale. There are multiple dimensions like this one, apparently. Our side knows them collectively as the Shade Planes. Home to the demons with which we arcane practitioners have been locked in a battle of our own doing for eons. While to us the various Shade Planes would look much the same, I am told there are some key differences. Something to do with a hierarchy, a pecking order.

I'd like this to be clear: the minutes of the meeting come from a most unreliable source. I have an extract detailed below, as it was reported to me.

Take it with a pinch of salt. I know I did.

You have something of mine...

A FELLOW DARKLING. I HAD SENSED YOUR PRESENCE.

Well done, I guess.

I WAS THE FIRST TO MAKE THE CROSSING IN A LONG TIME. I HAD NOT HEARD OF ANY OTHERS DO THE SAME IN THE PAST COUPLE OF HUNDRED YEARS, IN THESE MORTALS' TERMS...

Congratulations, Gramps. Now give me back what is mine.

IRREVERENT PIPSQUEAK. THIS IS MY TURF! WHATEVER CRACK YOU SCARPERED THROUGH, I WILL BE SENDING YOU BACK SHORTLY. IN PIECES.

You are the one who'll be sent back.

THIS IS HIGHLY IRREGULAR. I WAS HERE FIRST!

Irrelevant. I'll be here last. And forever after.

Ominous pause (I am told).

WHICH KIND ARE YOU, PIPSQUEAK?

The new kind.

THE NEW WHAT?

The New Dark.

Something had changed.

My first hint came from a most unlikely source. My right pinkie.

It wriggled.

I tentatively flexed my ring finger, then my middle finger, all the way along to my thumb.

A moment later, Al confirmed my hunch.

I kicked him out. You're welcome.

My resident demon sounded rather chuffed with himself. I contemplated thanking him. Then I remembered how most of the terrible events in my life, including being in Elderstay in the first place, could be traced back to him.

The elation at having my body returned to me was immediately replaced by the urge to give it back. Being dumped all at once into the physical experience is not for the faint-hearted. While for some fuzzy stretch of time I had felt nothing but the weightless detachment of the ethereal part of me, now *everything* hurt. The pain my body experienced since the demon had made me its puppet was catching up with me. The pulled tendons and fatigued muscles, the sleep deprivation and pangs of hunger. It hit me all at once. My arms and legs were chafed raw and my neck was killing me. I must have been oxygen-deprived because my sight was blurry and my cheeks sore from all the crazed smiling I seemed to have been doing. I was like a barmaid in a seedy tavern at the end of a twelve-hour shift.

We don't have time to waste, Gerome. The demon of Elderstay knows you've broken free–

Al didn't have time to finish his sentence. The tendrils around my legs and neck loosened. My arms still bound, I was hauled up and swung at nausea-inducing speed through the air. When the world had stopped spinning, I found myself in front of a dead milky orb. The demon's eye was as big as me.

"IT SEEMS WE HAVE AN UNWANTED GUEST..."

This time the demon had used Polly to speak instead of me. Our connection had been severed. And the demon did not sound particularly happy about it.

The snake spat out Bijan and whisked its head towards its demon master, jaw still loose. It was a questioning expression. I hadn't realised snakes could have expressions. Questioning or otherwise. As for Bijan, currently writhing on the ground, I wish he'd stop screaming and go get his sword.

"I WILL HAVE TO MAKE DO WITHOUT YOU. PITY, WIZARDS ARE A DEMON'S FAVOURITE PLAYTHING..."

"Guys," I whined pitifully, "a little help?"

Out of the corner of my eye, I noted Bijan had gathered himself sufficiently to get to his feet. But it was obvious he'd be as much use as tits on a kipper. In the poor man's defence, he looked much like you'd expect of someone who'd been half swallowed by a gargantuan reptile: ashen-faced and slightly violated.

Polly was much the same as I had been. Unable to move, wearing a demented smile, and occasionally used in the demon's ventriloquist act.

I was on my own. Almost on my own.

Release me.

I can't! I won't!

Release me or you'll die!

You'll destroy the world!

So will the demon of Elderstay!

Our squabble was cut short as I was yanked so violently my arms were almost pulled clean from their sockets. Through watering eyes, I peered down – into the abyss of revolving teeth.

Cave lampreys. I was reminded of cave lampreys, an Underdwell delicacy. Very nice smoked, on a cracker with a piece of cheese. As a child, at the Saturday food market, I would inspect the deep recesses of their foul toothy mouths through the fishmonger's glass tanks.

I thought of them again, as I contemplated the swirling vortex of sharp fangs and bone-like splinters that lined the inside of Elderstay's demon. All the way down to its grisly unspeakable innards. I felt like I was staring at the doorway to the Shade Planes. Perhaps, I was.

Last chance, Gerome.

Damn it, Al, I said no —
The tendrils around my wrists came undone.
I fell.
Towards the slicing, ripping, slashing horrors below.
Fuck.
Me.

…

Chapter Ten

THE END OF EVERYTHING

Red.

Everything went red. The heat was like an exploding star. The roar of a blaze that could have levelled a forest. I watched – eerily detached and draped in a mantle of pure flame – as a crimson ball carved its way through the world beneath me, more formidable than anything I had ever conjured.

My casting hand. Extended before me with graceful composure. It seemed different. My fingers were long and slender, rather than stubby and calloused by years of blisters. I'd always been self-conscious about that. Decades of fire-wielding had toughened my palms to the consistency of a well-done steak.

I would have liked to check out my other appendages, but whoever was in charge had no time for my inquisitiveness. From my back-seat driver position, I realised a few things.

I was laughing. Not at anything in particular, as far as I could tell.

Also, I was flying. No – *worse* – I was hovering off the ground. A sudden terrifying image flashed before my eyes. Levitating while cackling like mad, peppering the world below with death and destruction. A power move that required levels of concentration and recklessness possible only to the utterly deranged or the insanely powerful. Or a little of both.

Oh, no.

This was the signature technique of every–

"EVIL WIZARD!"

The devastating fireball hadn't quite finished the job. Through the smoke and collapsing rubble, the demon-baby emerged. Its tendrils were ripping huge chunks of stone from the ceiling, the noise it was making like a flock of a thousand geese. I realised, with a bite of twisted satisfaction, half of the demon's mouth had been blown off. Foul goop was gushing from its wound, solidifying in misshapen lumps as it attempted to retain some vague semblance of structural integrity, and balance the severe dent that skewed one side of its body. Demons in their "natural" state are composed purely of destructive cha- otic energy. They love dishing pain out. Yet are sorely un- prepared when it comes to experiencing it themselves.

"YOU CHEATING PIPSQUEAK!"

I heard myself laugh like a madman. Not me, to be precise. I wasn't responsible for my actions anymore.

"Had enough, big boy?" I heard myself shout with cruel delight.

Not my choice of words.

Will you be quiet in there, Gerome?

The least I can do is comment. You – you stole me! From me!

I felt an evil grin stretch my lips.

You gave yourself up.

Oh, bollocks. Did I?

Al was right. As I was about to meet my grisly end, I had given in to my personal demon.

You know, dear reader, what *really* roasted my nuts? To keep Al in check, I had acquired an unhealthy addiction to three distinct substances. Cut ties with my family. Lost my job, and my lover. My whole life was flushed down the toilet. All of it, to keep a demon locked up and the world safe. Just to throw it all away because I couldn't handle being minced alive, demon style.

Not much I could do about it now. Except enjoy my front-row seat for doomsday.

I made the most of it. The casual glimpses I got through Al's eyes revealed Polly slumped on the ground. When the fireball had blasted through the monster's face, it had dropped her from a considerable height. There was a dribble of blood oozing from her temple. The demon wouldn't be using her to speak anytime soon.

I would have wanted to check on Polly, but Al didn't appear to care for that idea at all. In another glance, I spotted the flash of a greatsword. I felt a joyous whoop in whatever parts still belonged to me. Bijan was alive. So alive in fact, he was attempting to hack at Sha-sha. The snake was hissing at him without enthusiasm, eyes locked on its demon-baby master. Suddenly, its thin reptilian lips parted open. The demon's spine-tingling words seemed hauntingly apt in the mouth of a giant serpent.

"YOU THINK YOU CAN STOP ME?"

The gargantuan demon began to shudder like a jelly pudding. The mustard glow surrounding us appeared to grow more intense.

Let's finish this, shall we?

I felt myself glide upwards, high above the sounds of combat and the smashing of falling rocks. A thick, dark energy was flowing inside of me, rippling through my aura. A heat like I had never dreamed of conjuring. Two incandescent nuggets of flame swirled in my handsome and hydrated hands. The energy was like nothing I had ever experienced.

What are you doing?

Your fireball is child's play. I am going to show you its true version...

I felt whatever was left of me go cold to the core.

The Suprema Sphaera Ignis.

It was but a rumour among elemental casters. Relegated to impenetrably written specialist papers on arcane lore, stored safely within purpose-built enchanted vaults beneath considerable amounts of stone and dirt. Any academic symposiums where the *Suprema* might be mentioned were by invitation only. Attending required the participants to pledge a vow of silence and have a letter of recommendation penned by the rector of a prominent magical university. And, even under these circumstances, the *Suprema Sphaera Ignis* was only ever discussed on a theoretical basis. Even talk of attempting the *Suprema* in anything other than an environmentally controlled pocket of no-space could cost you your arcane practitioner's licence, and land you in trouble with the Enchanted Institution. It was world-ending magic. It could level a city. At the right angle and with enough willpower, it might blast through the earth's core and blow up the planet. Aim it at the sky, and it might burn off the atmosphere. Target some poor sub-dimension and said dimension might blink out of existence, as if it'd never been. The number of witches and wizards who could summon a sufficient amount of raw potential energy to attempt it could be counted on one hand. And all had been banned from ever using it.

No. I couldn't let this happen.

Al, I'm begging you, no! There are reasons it's forbidden magic! You'll kill everyone. And I mean everyone!

And why do you think I'd care?

The nuggets of heat enlarged, swirling at the centre of my palms like little marbles of extermination. We weren't the only ones getting ready for havoc. The demon-baby was glowing. The light from the sickly goo that lined the walls and ceiling had begun to seep back towards the monster in long yellowish rivulets. I watched as the malignant energy swirled back to its master. The very same that had formed the barrier around Elderstay. Now, through Al's eyes, I knew what I was looking at.

No magic is created or destroyed. The first rule of magical dynamics. This was the life force of the people of Elderstay. The demon hadn't killed them. It had sucked them dry and left their empty husks to roam. Their essence had not been allowed to cross whatever veil separates the living and the dead, to be with their god, or dissipate in the infinite magnitude of All That Is. Take your pick, I'm a wizard, not a theologian. The demon had kept what made the city's inhabitants alive. Some would say, their very souls. This impressed Al as much as it disgusted me. But now was not the time for moral debates. I could sense it. The demon-baby was gathering itself for an attack. The huge milky eye in the middle of its face began to shine ominously.

"GO ON, PIPSQUEAK."

"Old demons first, Gramps," teased Al through my lips.

While the two fiends sized each other up, in the same fashion men discreetly assessed the bulge in each other's trousers, I noticed something. I got the distinct feeling Al hadn't. And neither had the demon-baby.

Polly.

The girl had forced herself to her feet. Her leg was bent at a funny angle, and she was dragging it along the ground in what must have been an excruciating exercise of willpower. She was limping towards the false altar and the rusted helmet – Lighthelm. I would have liked to follow her movements. But Al was keeping my eyes firmly on his adversary. A second later, she had vanished from our range of vision. I prayed that Polly had a plan. From some remote part of the underground hall, I could hear the fierce clashing of metal on scaly flesh and a snake making furious hissing noises. But worrying about Polly and Bijan was proving more difficult with every passing moment. My handsome hands were burning so bright they were practically incandescent. I was reaching the limits of my magical abilities. Al was surpassing them. But even he was approaching capacity.

I felt Al's grin widen in sick enjoyment.

My cue.

The blaze erupted from my extended hands, propelled towards the demon-baby. In the same instant, a jet of mustardy light blazed from its milky eye.

This was the end of the road. The end of everything.

Then I saw it.

A glint. As if in slow motion, a rusty helmet soared through the air as Al's supreme fireball and the monster's death beam hit.

A shard of purest light between two colliding forces of darkness.

I would never know how Polly did it. Perhaps Mushy helped adjust the helmet's trajectory. Or it was simply a mind-blowing, gobsmacking, once-in-a-lifetime golden stroke of luck. All I know is, if someone had to replicate the serendipitous throw, they could have tried a million times without achieving its timely perfection. As both demonic blasts struck the helmet, I realised a few things.

First off, time dilated. I am not sure if this was just for me, because when you don't have a body perception somewhat changes.

Secondly, where the Lighthelm met the colliding nefarious energies, a rip in the fabric of existence had opened. I was not certain where it came from or where it might lead. All I knew was that it was spewing white light, a luminescence so pure the darkness never stood a chance. I felt Al melt from my body. Like a cleansing wave, washing away the demonic sludge that fouled my soul. The Harbinger of the New Dark was yanked clean out of me. I had no time to feel relief, however, as I realised a third and final thing.

I was going to die.

The erupting light was followed by a blade of incandescent radiance. A purging force of such intensity, it would have disintegrated any living creature, demonic or otherwise, within its radius. Al and I had been hovering mere feet from the impact.

I made up my mind in a fraction of a nanosecond. Retrospectively, this decision does not make me look particularly good.

A lot of history has been written by the people who fled, rather than those who fought.

I was planning on writing a lot of history.

Ping.

On some transdimensional level, I felt an eruption of energy ripple across the known cosmos. Nestled in no-space, in my comfortable ten-by-ten personal storage unit – filled with all kinds of cherished belongings and downright junk – for the first time in a long time, I was alone.

Al?

I waited for him to answer. I couldn't afford to feel relieved, to feel anything at all. My apprehensive heart was beating like mad, while my mind raced to come to grips with what I had witnessed.

A god had died.

Taking two demons with it.

The resulting explosion had been cataclysmic.

I may have saved myself, but there was no knowing what had happened to the others. Polly. Bijan… The power of the blast would have cracked every bone in their bodies and boiled the blood in their veins – no. I was not going to think that. I was going to think happy thoughts – no. That wasn't working, either. The only way I had ever known to distract my overactive mind was by solving a puzzle. I had one conveniently at hand. I began wading through the mess of personal paraphernalia and litter I had stashed in my bachelor pad in no-space, pinching my chin as I paced up and down.

Polly had destroyed the Lighthelm. The sacred relic that had been gifted to her ancestor, Agris, by an ancient god worshipped by Lord Edmund and, I assume, everyone else in Elderstay. A god her father had turned his back on in favour of anyone who might breathe life into his dead child. The demon had replaced that faith. More tangibly, the physical manifestation of that faith: the helmet. Demons don't belong in our dimension. They need to have been allowed in, either on purpose or – and I knew this only too well – by accident. But more than anything, they needed something or someone to anchor them once here. I think I understood: the helmet had been the demon's anchor. If the god's last relic, the Lighthelm, were to no longer exist, the demon had lost its lifeline to our world.

As to how, exactly, the demon had slipped into a dead baby by filling a vacuum left by the Lighthelm? The answer had to be in the ingredients. Bring together unspeakable grief, a desecrated holy relic, and a string of demonic chants in a place of worship, and it's bound to go wrong. It was subtle stuff at work. Lord Edmund's actions, but more than that – his loss of faith – had allowed a demon to find a tear between our side and theirs.

I wondered where Lord Edmund, a former church-goer, might have learned the dark supplications I'd heard him mutter in the cathedral, as he'd stooped over his lifeless baby. The sad truth was that there were plenty of half-witted demon worshippers in Tellarin. More so now than ever before. It was a quietly accepted notion in the magical community that our gods were dead or dying. Hardly any superior being seemed to be watching over us, let alone want to have anything to do with us. The populace still clung on to their old idols and images of saints and deities, but the higher-ups in their lofty towers knew this was the naivety of children. We had been witnessing the light vanish from our world for a while. There were new philosophies, brewing in the minds of the cultured and magically inclined. Dangerous philosophies, in my opinion. Views that claimed witches and wizards, with our penchant for the arcane and exceptional intellects, were the ones destined to take on the mantle of our gods. Ludicrous stuff. If my peers were anything to go by, the average magic caster had as much common sense as a bread roll.

I considered my own demon dilemma. I had been the one to open a breach for Al. Like the Lighthelm for the

Elderstay demon, I was Al's anchor to this world. Yet, I was still alive. I checked myself again to make sure. But Al had been destroyed. Can demons be obliterated? The first rule of magical dynamics would suggest not. He must have been propelled back to the Shade Planes then. Or wherever else he claimed to have come from. Me here, and him there. The balance was restored; all pieces of the puzzle slotted back into their proper place...

All this thinking was making my brain hurt and was best left for a time when I'd had a bath, a warm meal, and a full night's sleep. It would be nice to have those again. The last thing I ate was a nail-sized mushroom and a mouthful of demon goop.

No point hanging around here.

Polly. Bijan. The world.

I had to go back for them.

As Damian, brother number one, would have said: it was time to face the music.

I reappeared in complete darkness. The mustardy glow from the slime on the walls, which had been the primary source of light in the bowels of the earth beneath Lighthelm Cathedral, had vanished.

I flicked a controlled bright-bolt on spin mode. A little trick I had picked up from my very first arcane teacher, a sour-faced elf by the name of Wilhelmina Van Stridden.

I blew on it. The spinning glow flew up towards the ceiling and hung in mid-air like a tasteful piece of essentialist homeware, illuminating much of my surroundings. I began walking cautiously about the underground hall, fretful at what I may find.

First, I spotted the outline of a massive hill in the dark. With fierce relief, I realised it was Sha-sha. Dead. The Lighthelm's blade of light had severed the snake clean in half. The flash of unstoppable radiance appeared to have travelled horizontally through the air, emanating from the point of impact, rather than exploding. This had been lucky for those on the ground. Not so much for anyone positioned high enough to be hit. That would have included me, had I still been floating about the ceiling. Judging by the sword dug deep in the middle of the snake's massive head, Bijan wasn't taking any chances. Speaking of the champion, I spotted a glint of armour in the glow of my spinning bright-bolt. Bijan was leaning against his kill, his eyes closed and his breathing shallow. His head turned weakly to look at me. He raised a finger in my general direction, an accusatory one. His lips moved unintelligibly. I supposed it was something about my heritage or my mother's chosen vocation, I couldn't quite hear him. Thankfully, he seemed too exhausted to do much more to me.

I proceeded past Bijan, towards where the false altar had been. The malevolent feeling. The taste of strawberries. It was gone. Of the demon-baby and its foul aspic body, there was no trace. As if it had never existed. A mistake on the linear time-continuum which had been duly noted by the forces that be and rectified; wiped clean from our reality, leaving nothing behind except...

Oh.

A baby. The goop had vanished, replaced by bare, cold rock in the gloom of the underground. The baby was atop it, unscathed. As if it had died merely a few hours before. Untouched by the decade of evils that had befallen its birthplace. I kneeled beside the newborn and closed my eyes. It felt like the right thing to do. I am not religious; I am of the school of thought that there is magic and logic, and both work by determinate measurable laws. I will stick to what can be proven rather than wishful thinking. I'd forge my own path rather than place my salvation in the hands of a bunch of inattentive, unfathomable entities. But I do believe that nothing that had once existed ever truly disappeared. Now, at least, the Lady and Lord's son would be free to transit into whatever existence lay beyond death. As, I assumed, the rest of Elderstay's walking corpses would.

A sudden whimper made my aching heart leap with relief.

Polly. She was crumpled on the ground. You didn't need to be a doctor to know she would require medical help. Alas, I had never taken those kinds of arcane papers at university. Conjuring fire had always been the way to impress the boys, not healing magic. Even if knowing some curative arcana and medicinal remedies would have helped with all the burns I'd acquired throughout my career.

Standing there, looking down at the girl who had dragged me through this ordeal – with little concern as to my wellbeing, or that of anyone else along the way – I could not help but feel a pang of pity. The eldest daughter of the rulers of Elderstay. Who had lost her mother to childbirth and her brother too. Who had watched her father be torn apart by a demon and her city trapped beneath a demonic yellow dome. Who had been raised by a Leshi in a cave, removed from the warmth and complexities of urban social living. As far as I was aware, she hadn't had the chance to go to school, have friends, or fall in love. Polly had never had the opportunity to do much at all. When a demon had started speaking to her under the guise of being her long-lost father, Lord Edmund, how could she have known any better? I knew how convincing a demon could be. All anyone would see was the girl covered in sickly spores who had betrayed her companions and aligned herself with a demon. If Bijan didn't kill her, Brent would. Niece or not, I doubted he'd care. The greedy lord of Snowden wanted Elderstay. He'd probably like the idea of getting rid of its natural heiress. Even if – because of odd human hang-ups – she would not inherit the city, it would be the scaffold for her. And for me too, if word got out about my tangled role in this messy affair.

"They won't understand," I muttered to no one in particular.

I placed my hand on Polly's. Her black eyes flickered, finding mine in the half-light.

"Gerome…?"

I thought of the sun's warm touch on my skin. Of how the dawn light might shimmer off the water's surface, peppering me with sparkles. Of my fingertips, as they hovered above the plethora of multicoloured goldfish and their elegant swirling tails, their mouths skimming the rimmed edge of the fountain for morsels of food. That should be enough.

"Let's go."

Bizzap.

Chapter Eleven

UNCOMFORTABLE TRUTHS

Polly and I reappeared by the fountain, outside Lighthelm Cathedral. I made a triumphant whooping sound. I hadn't been able to use short-distance teleportation for almost a year. It was as far as I dared go without forgetting easily overlooked stuff like clothes or fingers. It was routine wizard material. To be perfectly honest, it's the reason most of us are a little soft around the edges. Why walk anywhere, when you can *bizzap* up the stairs, or to the letterbox and back? I had gotten used to doing without many of my former talents. The perpetual presence of drugs in my system had made teleportation rather unsavoury. Partridge had gotten sick of finding me stark naked at the bar, when I would teleport down the stairs for a drink. Apparently, I was startling the patrons. There was *a lot* to be startled about.

I took a deep breath. My lungs filled with the crisp morning air. The sun was peeking over the horizon, painting my overgrown hair in varying shades of the colour "carrot". I turned back and noticed Polly was staring at me from her prone position. As if she'd never quite seen me before.

"You looked different, back there," she commented, straightening herself up against the edge of the fountain.

"How so?" I asked, a tad evasively.

"When you were flying and laughing like a maniac. You looked," she struggled for the right word, "*great.*"

"Honey, I always look great."

I kneeled beside Polly to check her leg. The spores didn't seem inclined to let me. They were assembling around her swollen limb in what I could only assume was an attempt to assist. Remarkably, her leg was looking better already.

"Whatever, Gerome. What I meant is, you looked… perfect."

There was no point in covering up the truth. My physical changes hadn't been relegated to my hands alone. I knew better than anyone what Al looked like.

"Let me guess," I said, without meeting her eyes. "I was an eleven out of ten? Tall, impeccably proportionate, smoking hot? Luscious red hair that fell with effortless grace over a pair of mesmerising green eyes? Chiselled cheekbones, straight white teeth, a firm sculpted butt, and – overall – the smouldering good looks of a god?"

"Something like that," muttered Polly, a tad self-conscious. Al had obviously triggered the girl's puberty.

"That was my demon. Al, the Harbinger of the New Dark. He's gone now. When the Lighthelm exploded – inspired move by the way, Polly, well done – my demon left my body."

I wasn't quite sure how to interpret the expression on Polly's face. She looked almost disappointed. Or, better, confused.

"But demons are malevolent, twisted beings. Like the horrible mound of talking goo we just faced. What Al looked like was just – wow."

"Just *wow*, huh?" I grinned at her playfully and straightened up, turning back to Lighthelm Cathedral.

"Where are you going?" Polly said to my back.

"I have to go get Bijan. It's going to take him hours to crawl out of there by himself. I owe him that much. And an explanation about his brother. I would advise you not to be in sight when we do come back," I added. "He'll likely blame you too, for what happened."

There was a long pause. I could feel her stare, searing in between my shoulder blades.

"You're not coming back, are you?"

"I am not sure where you'll go from here, Polly," I said, dodging her question. "But, if I were you, I'd give Snowden a wide berth. Especially Lord Brent. And the goblins. And the humans too. Just stay away from everyone."

"You said you'd tell me about your demon 'later'. Now's *later*."

"I'm pretty sure I never said that," I countered.

"Why don't you stay and tell me about Al?"

"Polly," I growled in my lecturer voice. "Are you trying to keep me here?"

I turned back to her. She was wearing a peculiar expression but said nothing.

I had never told anyone this story. I guessed I could spare a minute.

As embarrassing as it may be for me, Polly might soon be the only one who'd know the truth about how Al came to be in my life.

"You promise to hear me out?" I asked. "Till the end?"

She nodded enthusiastically.

"And you won't laugh?"

"Why would I laugh?" Polly noticed my face and added, "Okay, I won't laugh. I swear." She crossed her heart, in what I had to assume was the human version of a pinkie promise.

"As you may have heard me mention once or twice, I was a junior lecturer at the Arcane Polytechnic in Grandfall. One of thirteen brothers – all boys, bless Mother's soul – I was the only one of my family to venture far from home. I was a happy-go-lucky kind of guy with a winning smile and a tad too much talent for my own good. Like a fish to water, I immediately took to the big city. Grandfall had a nightlife and career prospects. I got to mingle with kindred spirits in my field of magic and focus on my research. They called me

'Professor Gerome'. Not bad for some gnome sprog from the backwaters of Underdwell… Everything was going swimmingly. Then, *bam*! The worst thing that could have ever happened to me…"

"What happened?"

"I fell in love."

My lips curled involuntarily. The warmth was but a glimmer of its former self. But still there. It was always still there.

"I had been in my job for a few months when I got an invitation to a dinner party. A fancy event at the Department of Abjuration. On that fateful night, I met him."

Polly's eyes widened. *"Him?"*

I hesitated. "Is this going to be a problem?"

"No. It's just… most people keep that stuff to themselves."

"Do you want to hear the rest of the story, or not?"

Polly nodded again.

I cleared my throat. This was harder than I'd thought. "His name was Constantine Ovalis Galbraith. Deputy-head of the most exclusive arcane establishment in the world, the Floating Faculty. He had me from the moment he glanced my way. We started a torrid and *discreet* love affair. One that threatened to ruin me in more than one way. While I was head over heels for Constantine, I sensed I was never quite enough for him."

"In what way?"

"Polly, you promised you'd let me finish."

I waited for her to nod again before continuing. "All you need to know is that there are some physical differences between humans and gnomes. Differences I felt I needed to make up for. Let's leave it at that. So, one day, in Constantine's office, I tried to – ehm – *improve* myself. Unfortunately, I... I opened a rift." I tried to ignore Polly's eyes, as wide as saucepans at this point. "A demon, unlike any that has ever crossed over before, possessed me. The demon claimed to be the Harbinger of the New Dark. A novel kind of demon that would succeed where all others had failed thus far..."

"... failed to do what?" asked Polly.

"To end the world."

I allowed a moment for my words to sink in. "I discovered early on that some substances could keep Al in check. Psychoactive substances. Good thing he's gone now. I'm not sure how much longer my liver could take the abuse." I chuckled, in a vague attempt to make light of one of the most tragic predicaments the planet had faced for over a millennium.

There was silence. The longest, most judgemental silence I had ever been subjected to.

"You got possessed by a demon... because you wanted to magic yourself a bigger codpiece?"

That summed it up. Except it didn't.

"I know it sounds ridiculous."

"A rift to the Shade Planes to do *that*? How did you even manage it?!"

"I don't know." Another reason I hated this statement so much. I really didn't know. The personal modification of one's anatomy is a relatively common transmutation spell. I mean, I was hardly the first wizard who'd done it. While this is kept strictly off the arcane history books, I am willing to bet a sizeable sum of money that penis enlargements were one of the very first alteration charms ever performed. Turning into a fish or a bird, my ass.

True, transmutation is a tricky discipline, and not my area of expertise. It takes decades to master. Constantine was very proficient in that kind of thing. I'd found the basic spell in *Fundamentals of Appearance*, a first-year arcane textbook, in his office, where I'd been waiting for him. It was his birthday, and I'd wanted to surprise him as he'd been acting aloof. More than usual, anyway.

I'm not sure what went wrong. Perhaps, that regrettable night, the barrier between dimensional planes had been thinned by some mysterious galactic phenomenon. Maybe it had been how I was feeling in my heart, my motives. A bit too much vanity, perhaps? Or far too much desperation?

I found my throat constricting.

"I just wanted Constantine to love me."

Polly looked at me. And the way she did confirmed everything I had always known. I felt so silly. So deeply silly. The silliest man of all races, in all times, in all eras past and present and whatever remained of the future to ever walk the earth. I had doomed all of existence to a slow demise into the shadowy dusk of eternity. For a man. A man who'd possibly never felt the same way I did. And, to this day, I wasn't even sure how I'd managed it.

"I really should get going."

"Wait!" On unsteady legs, Polly got to her feet. "Bijan is going to kill you."

"I murdered Najib."

That put an end to the argument. I lifted my hand to wave. I hadn't expected her to stagger forward and cup it between hers.

"In case you need it."

I opened my palm to find a nettle of fine white roots.

"What is it?"

"It's a mother mycelium. It'll sprout the orange mushrooms you like. Put it in a jar. Keep the jar moist and warm and it'll grow mushrooms daily. If you look after it with care, it'll never stop producing. Not that you'll need them if Al is gone for good. But you know. Recreational."

"Thank you, Polly." I wouldn't mind having a mushroom before facing Bijan. "So, where to for you now?"

She shrugged. "I might hang around here. I want to see if I can find Father's old piano. I'm rusty, but I have the time to practice… Seems like I'm going to miss out on my uncle's promise of land, titles, and riches."

"Oh, not the titles, milady." I bowed with flair. "To your good health, and farewell thee, Lady Polly of the House of Agris and Ruler of Elderstay."

I felt her hands tighten around mine, holding me in place a moment longer.

"Farewell, Gerome the gnome." Her black eyes were bright and alive, happier than I had ever seen her. She almost resembled that little girl I'd seen behind the pillar in Lighthelm Cathedral, before the demon arrived. Before all the deaths and the loss.

"Thank you, for helping me take back my home."

Bizzap.

The underground hall was as I had left it. My brightbolt was still spinning on itself, more languidly now. It would eventually implode and vanish without much fuss. Maybe another few minutes of light before I'd have to cast a new one.

I spotted Sha-sha's form in the dying glow. There was a grisly wound in the middle of her skull and a long rivulet of blood pooling beneath her slack jaw. The sword had been extracted. Ominous indeed.

"Bijan," I called, sweat pearling my forehead. "Bijan, I've come to get you out of here."

I heard the clanging of metal boots behind me. I felt something heavy and cold lie flat on my shoulder, grazing my exposed neck. In the corner of my eye, I spotted a silver glint, tarnished by darker streaks of dry blood. A sword.

"Kneel," growled Bijan, in a low voice.

"Bijan, I know you're angry—"

"I said *kneel*."

I did as I was told. I didn't dare teleport away. I hardly think I could have summoned the concentration necessary. It's hard to think about much with a blade at your throat.

"I found Najib," started Bijan, his voice drained of all emotion, "or what little was left of him. His armour had been scorched almost beyond recognition. Something no ordinary flame could have done. Something only one of us could. A wizard." I heard him draw a laboured breath. "Then I saw you flying. I saw you cast a fireball. The same kind that destroyed Najib. You didn't look like a gnome anymore. You had transformed into something else. Something wicked. I should have listened to my amulet. I should have known from how it was burning, that my worst fears about you were true. You *are* a demon."

"No… and yes."

"Which one is it?" The sword was no longer lying flat on my shoulder. Some deeply instinctive part of me knew it was hovering unseen, ready to take the swing.

"I had a demon in me, true. But he's gone now. He's gone, I swear it, Bijan! He was destroyed when the helmet exploded, the Lighthelm. I mean, I don't know what happened, but he's not here!" The threat of an imminent and fatal stroke was making me incoherent. "Almost a year ago, I accidentally tore a rift between dimensions. A demon entered my body. I was able to keep it imprisoned inside me, suppressing it the best I could. But it's gone now. I swear it is. I'm sorry… I should have told you."

There was a long pause.

"Was it you or your demon who killed Najib?"

The way he said his brother's name. I could barely speak, let alone lie. In my silence, Bijan drew his own conclusions. I felt him press the sharp metal against the nape of my neck, one last time.

"It is customary to grant final words," he breathed.

A shadow of a grin curled my lips. "I don't have any, off the top of my head."

I heard him repress a snort at my ill-timed levity. A sense of humour. I couldn't remember him having one of those. Aside from the fratricide business, we might have worked. That is, if Bijan had been at all interested in a fun-sized, unemployed drug addict. He probably wasn't of my same proclivity, anyway. It wasn't something people flaunted in these parts of the world.

"I'm sorry I killed your brother, Bijan."

I tried to keep my tears in check but failed.

I have twelve brothers. I have, on occasion, hated every one of them. Yet, if someone dared pluck a single hair off their heads, I would fireball them to a crisp, no questions asked. That's what having a sibling is like. Anyone who has one knows. I wanted Bijan to know that before he did what he had to.

"Najib wasn't my brother."

A lengthy silence stretched between us. Broken by me. Losing my mind.

"What?!"

I turned to face Bijan. In the dimming light from my bright-bolt, which cast long shadows down his face, I squinted at his appearance. I was relieved to see his sword arm had dropped to his side. Yet Bijan looked different. I couldn't have explained how exactly, but my eyes perceived subtle alterations in his visage, minor transformations that alone might have gone undetected but, together, painted the picture of a changed man.

"Najib was an *aayne*. A mirror."

"At the risk of repeating myself – what?!"

"When I was a boy, I was a bad child. A slow learner, prone to deceit and mischief, and other objectionable tendencies." His aquamarine eyes were boring into mine. "I struggled to read and write. I would not listen to my teachers and my betters. I preferred to play and dawdle, rather than apply my mind and learn the skills necessary to become a good and honourable man. My father, Sultan Khosrow the Magnificent, worried about me. He saw it, in his wisdom, to ensure that I would be an ideal successor after his death. The Sultan called upon many masters of science and sorcery to help me become a better version of myself. All that was base and evil about my personality was removed and placed in an empty armour. Here, all my darkness could be imprisoned, inert and harmless, in a hollow casing. The armour would be a mirror image of me, willing for nothing but to smite the evils of the world, as it contained mine. During the day, Najib would be an armour, and at night, a mirror. At day's end, I would peer into the mirror and pour in it all wicked thoughts, all foul desires. All that was imperfect and weak. To ensure I could find evil where it lurked, I was entrusted with an amulet – a piece of my *aayne*, Najib. So, whenever I doubted whether a thing was right or wrong, it would warn me." He distractedly touched the amulet dangling about his breastplate. I remembered the way he had stared at me back at the camp while holding it. It still gave me shivers.

"You detected my demon that night?"

Bijan nodded slowly. "When I looked at you, my amulet became so hot it burned me. But a moment later, it was cold and harmless, as if there was no evil in you at all. A rare thing. I assumed it had made a mistake."

"You had that trinket around your neck this whole time and you didn't pick up on Sha-sha? Wouldn't it go nova for someone like her?"

"Some can disguise themselves if they are hiding their true form. One must be discerning. The amulet goes warm at times, even with those you least expect it to. There are plenty of bad people out there…" Tears welled in his eyes. "Now, when I hold it for myself, I, too, sense its heat. Look at me, Gerome. What you have done to me!"

I did look at him. In the dying light, I was finally seeing it. His straight masculine nose had broadened, and his jawline was heavier. There were deep bags beneath his eyes that had not been there before, even in our most gruelling days. His thick curly hair fell limply around his face. But the changes were not merely in his appearance. I remembered how Bijan had always been fearless, whatever the stakes. Yet, in the battle with the demon-baby, he had been scared and hesitant. It was obvious he wanted to flee the battlefield. Like any other *normal* person. But Bijan was not meant to be a normal person.

What had made him the ideal champion was gone.

"I see *you*, Bijan. And don't you think this is who you were truly meant to be?"

Bijan made it clear he wasn't going to tolerate my platitudes. "When you destroyed Najib, all of my flaws returned to me! How am I meant to lead my people now? An imperfect sultan. A devious sultan!"

"We are all assholes as kids, Bijan. I was a right tyke. One of thirteen tykes, actually. Except for Damian. Damian was Mum's favourite. Anyway, to go and remove every trace of what your father deemed unsavoury about you, leaving all that he considered 'good'." I made sure to air quote the word. "That is a terrible violation. And not just a moral one. What your father did to you as a child sounds like forbidden magic, Bijan."

"You'd know, wouldn't you, *evil* wizard?"

I ignored the barb. I had to be certain. For my conscience's sake. "So, Najib was an empty case of armour? You never had a brother?"

"I did," muttered Bijan, in a hushed tone. "My older brother, Behzad, died a long time ago. In a skirmish with a neighbouring state. He was the one meant to take the throne and lead Sipera." It was sad to hear Bijan's bitterness. Like he resented his brother for dying on him.

We were silent. Me kneeling, him standing. Both of us unclear as to what we were supposed to do next.

"I should kill you," blurted out Bijan. "I'd be the first champion to ever vanquish a demon. I could go home. Bring your head as an offering to my father. He'd be so proud. He may even overlook my failings." Then, before I could argue, Bijan spoke again. The manic exhilaration in his voice had subsided to a demurer, almost defeated tone. "No. Just go. Get out of here. Lest I do something we will both regret…"

I got up slowly and gazed into the face of the Crown Prince of Sipera. Bijan looked so lost, so confused. I guessed the recovery of all that forcibly removed lifetime of negativity was doing a number on his psyche. It was as if more than one person dwelled within him. I knew how that felt. By destroying Najib, I might have given Bijan split-personality disorder.

No, not me, I reminded myself firmly. *His father. That's why forbidden magic is forbidden.*

"You're going to be okay, Bijan. Just like the rest of us – with a bit of darkness and a bit of light. You'll figure yourself out in all of it."

Suddenly, the champion pointed an infuriated finger at me. "I'm letting you go, this day. But be warned. Cross my path again, *gnome*, and I'll make you sorry you were ever born!"

"Bijan, I—"

"GET OUT!"

He began hacking at the air around him, maddened with anguish and fury. And, most likely, the mountain of emotional torment that had come crumbling down on him thanks to yours truly.

But, as my inner bastard reminded me (one which long predated Al), I had blasted a mirror to oblivion. I could not be put to death for smashing mirrors. Seven years of bad luck, sure. But being executed for breaking a mirror. *No siree, not me.* My relief was palpable. I felt a few inches taller. Without Al and the crushing burden of murder on my soul, I might dare to have my life back.

"I can give you a ride to the top. Or you can stay here and…" I watched Bijan slice at the walls until his sword shattered, "finish whatever it is you are doing."

He turned red-eyed towards me. The broken sword's hilt flew past my ear. I made up my mind. Bijan could find his own way out of here. Now that the slippery goo was gone, it'd be a long trudge but not an impossible one. At least, I thought, I'd get to Lord Brent before him. Hopefully, the shambolic tale of how we had defeated the demon of Elderstay – and my ambiguous role in all of it – would only reach the Lord in its entirety once I was halfway to Grandfall with my reward money safely stored in no-space.

I held Bijan's infuriated gaze. He still looked handsome to me, in a different way than before. A bit rougher around the edges. More melodramatic. And, maybe, a tad more accessible. Just about then, the bright-bolt blinked out of existence, plunging us into darkness.

I couldn't have said why, but I had a feeling this wouldn't be the last time we'd meet.

"See you around, Bijan."

Bizzap.

Chapter Twelve

HOMECOMING

I made it to Snowden around midday. I cut the journey short by teleporting myself along the snowy path whenever I had a clear view of what was in front of me. I would have been even faster, had I not gotten a little arcana-shy after I almost ported off a cliff. The morning had been graciously bright and fogless. It was as if the environment had perceived the energetic shift. The malice I detected on my way to Elderstay had vanished, the silence that seemed to drown all noise was gone. As were the strawberries on my tongue. The journey was blissfully tasteless and devoid of undead bodies. I'd even heard the odd bird chirping along the way. Yet something did nip at my soul.

Over fifty people had left Snowden, three days ago. Only one returned. I guess what Mum used to call me was true. I was a *lucky seven*.

I turned quite a few heads when I appeared at the keep's main gates. I avoided making eye contact. People immediately began to whisper at the sight of me, before rushing off to the alleyways that branched off the central courtyard. To alert more of Snowden's inhabitants to the return of this one "person of talent", no doubt. I pressed on to the Lord's residence, the Grand Hall, without stopping. I didn't want to have to answer uncomfortable questions about missing family members or friends. It had not sat well with me, what had happened to our squadrons. And I had a bone to pick with *Lord* Brent.

A couple of guards holding pikes stood at the door. They didn't ask for identification. Short, ginger, magical. My first arrival in Snowden must have left a lasting impression on the locals.

"Welcome back, sir gnome," said one.

Before they could add anything else, I grunted my thanks and entered the building, leaving the swelling crowd behind me. Though muffled through the thick wooden entrance, I heard the pike-holders shout out for people to disperse. I drew a breath of relief and took in my surroundings.

The Grand Hall was much as I remembered it. Stately yet pleasant, with a roaring blaze in the hearth and saturated with the smell of fatty meats on spits, wafting from one of the side kitchens. The Lord was clearly unafraid of gout. The vast hall appeared to be deserted, except for four figures scattered around the rambling room. A cursory glance suggested that one was a maid, unless this particular woman took enjoyment from dusting down mantelpieces; a couple of uniformed guards stationed in the corners; and a bespectacled elderly human sitting at a desk by the fireplace, perusing through documents and mouthing the end of a quill.

The maid glanced my way, and her rosy cheeks swelled with an exaggerated gasp. "Oh, goodness gracious! You've been through a mighty lot, sunshine, I can tell. You smell the part." Her tone was so disarmingly affable, I took a moment to realise she had said I looked like crap and stank too. "I'll go fetch Lord Brent for you. Then I'll go get you some nice rabbit soup so we can pump some warmth back into those chilly bones."

I was too drained to speak but gave her a grateful nod. It was one of the least challenging interactions I'd had of late.

The maid thumped up the stairs in her wooden clogs. A fashion choice I was willing to forgive, if soup was still on the table.

"Lord Brent, one of your *special* people is here!" I heard her shrill voice reverberate from upstairs.

I sank into a nearby seat. I thought back to when I had first set foot in the Grand Hall. It felt like an eternity ago. I remembered exactly where each of us had been positioned around the room. The dark corner where Polly had lurked. The table where the towering champions in their silver armour had been stationed. I eyed the chair in which Sha-sha had been awkwardly coiled. An icy shudder went down my back. More than anything or anyone else – demon-babies included – she, I would like to forget.

A minute later, I heard heavy footsteps descend the stairway, in the wake of the Lord's booming voice.

"Ah, you're back! So, did you deal with the – oh, Gerome!" He stopped dead, his red cloak whipping around his ankles.

I had the distinct impression Lord Brent had not expected to see me. He had expected to see *someone*. But that someone had not been me. *Interesting*.

We stared at each other for a long moment before Brent shot me an amicable smile, as if I were an old friend he'd been dying to catch up with. "Gerome, welcome back to Snowden! I am thrilled to see you safe and sound. Now, do tell! Has Elderstay been cleansed of the evil?"

"Oh, yes."

"So, the barrier and the walking corpses? Vanquished for good?"

"The magical dome is gone. The undead are properly dead."

"And the demon?"

I eyed Lord Brent's gleeful expression with a solid dose of hostility. He hadn't even asked me the whereabouts of my fellow companions. Or the squadrons he'd recruited to assist us. An insistent niggle in my brain suggested he had not expected any of us to come back.

Or, I thought darkly, *he made a deal with one of us to ensure the others didn't make it back.*

There was only one individual, among Brent's five "people of talent", whom I believed would have been well suited for such a task. Thankfully, she was lying in pieces at the bottom of a devastated cathedral with a foot-long incision in her head.

"Oh, the demon's gone alright. As is Sha-sha," I added, feeling a frown crease my forehead.

"That's a pity." Lord Brent grinned with what I could only assume was an expression of sincere relief. For the demon or Sha-sha, that part was unclear.

I shouldn't have been surprised. There were very few downsides to sending a bunch of thrill-seeking adventurers after a near-invincible foe. If we failed, it would be no skin off his nose. All he'd lose was the handful of gold coins he'd given each of us to stock up on supplies. If we succeeded, he got a city. Plus, you'd hardly expect everyone to come back intact, with what he knew was lurking behind Elderstay's barrier. Yes, Lord Brent hadn't gambled much to take back his brother's cursed city. Aside from a few dozen peasants from Snowden and a similar number of inconvenient goblins, whom he also hadn't had to pay. A sacrifice he was willing to make, I suppose.

"A lot of people died to open the barrier and buy us the time to enter Elderstay. A lot more people died in the city, at the demon's hands." I glared at his expression. "There is very little to smile about."

"Their deaths were for a noble cause, be sure."

I allotted the man a nasty stare. "Happen to know Bellamy Kirt's wife?" I stooped down to retrieve the pieces of folded parchment I'd stuffed in my boot. "I have a letter for her. Her husband wrote it before he died. I think his brother should read it too."

Brent clicked his fingers. A moment later, the maid who had greeted me approached His Lordship with an obsequious bow. She didn't appear to be as unimpressed as I was by the fact that she'd been summoned like a dog.

"Figure out who this should be going to, Margaret," he grumbled at the maid, handing her Mr Kirt's final report without even glancing at the words scribbled on the paper.

I watched as the woman scanned the missive, her lips pursed and her eyebrows knitted tight together. With a solemn curtsy to Lord Brent and a passing nod to me, she sprinted from the hall, her heavy clogs clicking in her wake.

Brent returned his attention to me. I did not like the way his eyes had narrowed. "So, Gerome, I trust you want your reward?"

"That would be nice. Land, titles, and riches, to be precise."

"Well, you can take your pick of a plot of land outside the keep. A full acre. A very generous offer."

"You mean the frozen, barren wasteland outside Snowden? An acre of it? All for me? Oh, goodie."

"It's very productive in potato season, I must say. And you are hereby a titular Baron of Snowden. Soon people will be calling you the *Vanquisher of Demons* and the *Cleanser of Elderstay*."

I wasn't too sold on those appellatives, either. "And the money, Brent?"

The Lord scowled, presumably at how his title had slipped off the edge of my sentence. "Right to the point, I see, gnome."

I detected a shift in our little spar. One that may result in me not seeing the money I had been promised. And possibly a fiery hole in the ceiling, depending on how I felt about that. I noticed the two guards at the edge of the hall hadn't taken their eyes off me.

An uneasy few seconds passed before Lord Brent muttered something rude to himself. He went up to a table at the end of the hall, placed discreetly in a more shaded corner where the lighting from the sconces didn't quite reach. On it was a small chest.

Brent beckoned me over and opened the chest with a key he'd had tied around his neck.

"A thousand gold pieces, as promised."

I eyed the contents of the chest. There were ten pouches. I peered inside a few to be sure. A hundred gold coins in each. I felt the weight of the pouches in my hands.

I was not a dwarf. Dwarves will get visibly, even carnally, aroused at the sight of gold. But I could get excited at the prospect of good food and drink. Of paying Partridge for putting up with me at the *Roaring Peacock* for as long as he had. Of buying new clothes and a decent pair of shoes. Of getting a haircut. A thousand gold pieces was just shy of an arcane lecturer's yearly salary. It was a lot of money. Yet, there was this troubling feeling I could not shrug.

"Funny," I said, eyeing one of the coins up close. "This chest contains a thousand gold coins, give or take a piece. The sum promised to each one of us *people of talent*. It's like you expected only one of us to return, Lord Brent."

A shadow crossed the Lord's face. I didn't need Bijan's amulet to imagine the kind of terrible suffering the human wished upon me.

"You will always be welcome here, Baron of Snowden. But now there is much to do. Elderstay awaits. You may stay the night if you wish. Or *not*."

With that, the Lord of Snowden and soon-to-be Lord of Elderstay left the hall, without another word. He'd done his business and discarded me like a smelly rag, which admittedly was an apt description for my current appearance. I was promptly waved down by the bespectacled elder at the desk. With a trembling hand, the old man handed me a certificate of title, complete with his notary scribble and the Lord's insignia, and a scrolled-up piece of parchment which contained my honorary title as Baron. I wondered if Professor Gerome, Baron of Snowden was a bit long. But B.o.S. Professor Gerome had a nice ring to it. The money would prove more difficult to carry. When a guard glanced my way, far too eagerly for my liking, I grinned and said, "Don't mind me, I'll put this somewhere safe."

Placing both hands tightly around the chest's handles, I blinked into no-space. My personalised ten-by-ten-feet pocket dimension was much as I'd left it. I waded through the mess of books and junk I'd tossed carelessly about the place and never bothered tidying up, and found the only unoccupied corner in the chaos. It was where I'd curl up to sleep, in case I didn't have a real bed at hand. I stuffed one of the hundred-coin pouches down my trousers and covered the chest with a smelly old blanket. I really needed to sort my shit out.

Having secured my veritable fortune in a place that existed only for yours truly, I blinked back to my last known location and trudged out of the Grand Hall. I'd been anxious of bumping into an agitated mob on my way out, but Lord Brent had spared me the burden. A crowd was assembling around the stables where a contingent of soldiers, headed by His Lordship, were busy mounting horses and loading gear, preparing to depart. Lord Brent was addressing the people clustered around him. His firm paternal voice rose above the quiet sobs and hushed mutterings. I could only catch a few words here and there, but it was clear he was taking all the credit for the liberation of Elderstay. Talk of noble sacrifice and necessary martyrdom.

I eyed the faces in the crowd lined with tears, looks of relief mingled with terrible grief. Of people who'd lost relatives and friends on the way to the cursed city. The demon was gone. But the cost had been steep. For us all.

Sick to my stomach, I kept walking. A minute or so later, I noticed a bunch of goblins loitering in the courtyard, at what seemed like a calculated distance from the crowd of humans gathered around Lord Brent. They were hissing in their harsh native tongue and casting filthy glares in His Lordship's direction. I recognised some of them as Polly's tent carriers.

"Hi," I said, lifting an appeasing hand as I approached them. My gesture was followed by some low-key snarling. One of them spat on the ground at my feet. I guessed Polly's poor behaviour had not been forgiven and very much *not* forgotten.

"One of 'em people of talent, yes-yes!" growled a she-goblin, arms crossed in front of her chest. "Gerome the gnome, innit, yes-yes?

A few of them sniggered at her lacklustre remark.

"Never gets old," I muttered flatly. "Look, did you know Bingop-ul? Did he have any relatives, a wife, or something else, perhaps?"

A dark silence fell upon the goblins. When the she-goblin spoke again, there was a quiver in her voice. "He was a *permgre*! Everyone knew Bingop-ul."

"Well, you guys take this. From Bingop-ul. Celebrate his life."

I reached inside my trousers and counted out five gold coins. Enough for a three-day bender at an establishment of their choice. Goblins or not, anyone would let them in with that kind of money.

They eyed me greedily. "You're bein' nice to us. Why?"

I gave a meek shrug. Maybe I was compensating for something. Something like having an apocalyptic force of darkness lodged in my brain for about a year.

"We should go enjoy it, while we can! We gotta leave soon," piped up the she-goblin, before I could come up with an answer.

"Why so?" I asked.

"If Elderstay's been freed and the Malicious One is gone, we're goin' back to the caves."

The others nodded in agreement. "Humans and goblins don't mix for long. The Lord said he wants us vacatin'."

I heard the audible chime of an idea go off in my head.

"How would you fancy having your very own piece of Snowden?"

"What'd you mean?"

"I happen to have an acre of land outside Snowden's keep. I'd be happy to hand it over to you."

"Uh? What for?"

"Oh, I don't know… Maybe to establish a permanent goblin embassy with easy access to your human allies. It'd be all yours, legally speaking. See the insignia? All official. Just a thought. What's your name?"

"Gum-ul," replied the she-goblin.

I magically shifted the letters in my name to hers and handed back the scroll. "Have fun."

I wished I could have seen Brent's face when he found the local goblin tribe had crammed themselves into an acre of land outside his bedroom window. Pity I'd be long gone by then.

Their beady eyes contemplated me for a moment longer, an unexpected glint of quiet gratitude in their skittish stares. "We'll drink to your good health, Gerome the gnome. And you'll have friends in goblins. We don't forget people that give us land."

"And booze!" cried another.

There were a bunch of assenting noises. It was true. Goblins had never been land-grabbers. They eked out an existence on the fringes of other societies, unable or unwilling to carve out their own. They made do with the places no one else wanted to live in. Dumpsters and caves.

"You should come join us for a drink!"

"Many thanks, but I can't stay." I had consumed enough alcohol and drugs in the past year to last me a lifetime. "But raise a glass to Bingop-ul for me."

I peeled away from the group of thrilled goblins and waved down a cart driver in the courtyard. I recognised him as the same ill-tempered man who'd brought me here from Grandfall.

"You want a ride?" grouched the cart driver, his lumpy face creasing with irritation. "It's going to cost you. I wasn't planning on making another trip till tomorrow."

"Will this suffice?" I put five gold coins in his hand. A little over a month's wages for a commoner.

I had never seen the grumpy northerner smile so broadly.

"Get comfortable, sir," he said as I climbed into the cart. "Ready to head back to Grandfall, I take it?"

"Oh, yes. With haste."

I turned to see Lord Brent mounting a powerful-looking steed. A pale creature which appeared remarkably similar to the white horses Najib and Bijan had ridden into Snowden. Brent's troop of soldiers were armed and falling into formation. He wasn't wasting any time. I silently wondered if he'd encounter Bijan on his way to Elderstay. A part of me regretted the poor champion would likely not see a single coin for all his troubles.

I heard the driver click his tongue, followed by the clipping of hooves on stone. I leaned back in the uncomfortable wooden seat, pulling my tattered coat around myself. I was spent. Starving. And my body odour would have put a cave troll to shame. But I was going back to Grandfall. I was loaded. I was demon-less. It was a long shot but I might be able to beg the Polytechnic to give me back my job. No one wanted to lecture elemental manipulation. It took a degree of bravery to stand in a room full of inexperienced and overeager students practising the art of fire-wielding. I could finally see my family in Underdwell. Maybe I'd write a letter to Constantine. Ask how he was doing. Ask if he ever thought of me…

I was buzzing. The prospect of having my life back. Of no longer needing the drugs. And no Al in my mind, wanting to take control at any moment. I felt Polly's nettle of mushroom roots in a jar against my breast and smiled. I hoped she was feeling as good as I was. Because that's what I was feeling for the first time in forever.

Good.

I leaned back and closed my eyes.

Suddenly, I was upright again, my heart in my throat.

Missed me, little man?

Oh… bollocks.

EPILOGUE

Shards here. Shards there. Shards a little bit everywhere.

The shards may have contemplated their life as it came to a close. After all, they'd had no business living. Life was something that had been thrust upon them. When they'd been whole. When they'd been named…

These might have been Najib's considerations, if the scattered remains that had once made up the mirror's physical presence had been able to *think* altogether. Let's assume they had. And what might the fallen champion have thought as it lay in a hundred half-molten pieces, strewn across a sprawling mosaicked plaza, shimmering in the light of the moon?

It would have thought it odd – to exist.

It is an even odder thing to *know* it existed.

To the self-contemplating mind, the universe does not make much sense.

It all starts to go wrong with the words: "I am…"

Specifically, the words, "I am Najib."

Such statements are soon followed by uneasy questions, such as: *What am I? Why am I here? Who made me? And, sooner or later, Is milkshake ice-cream soup?*

Before the name Najib, there had been none of this nonsense. Before being transformed into a six-foot-tall steel armour, that is. It had just been an *aayne*, a mirror. A surface coated with a metal amalgam designed to reflect an image.

A mirror's life is not exciting. Not as much as, say, that of a boot on an adventurer's foot, or that of a raunchy magazine in a brothel's waiting room. The mirror's purpose was simple: it mirrored. The world and its contents have a colour, a depth, an identity. A mirror does not. A mirror's function is to show, but not be seen. No one ever looks upon a mirror. They see only themselves. As it should be.

The mirror's existence had started in a faraway land, many hundreds of miles from where it lay now, shattered into pieces. In the sultanate of Sipera. Had the mirror had much use at the time for physical senses, it would have remembered Sipera as hot, dry, and full of red velvet drapes. Here, the mirror had spent much of its inert and uneventful existence in low light conditions, being exposed to individuals in various stages of undress. For many years, the mirror had done a good job, a mirror's job. It had witnessed hundreds of naked buttocks, and had numerous close encounters with squeezed pimples and suspicious warts.

Until the day it first uttered the words: "I am Najib."

It all started when two servants had entered its chamber and picked the mirror up by the sides, leaving oily fingertips on its lucid surface. The mirror was carried down a long corridor and into a cramped chamber. The room was dusky, lit only by the flickering glow of a handful of candles, and the air was thick with the potent scent of Siperan incense. Here, the mirror reflected the shadowy faces of three figures. A man. A boy. And a woman.

The man had a white beard and a prominent hat, eyes that seemed never to blink, and a mouth that likely seldom formed any expression other than contempt. The mirror had encountered enough members of the royal family to recognise the type. As for the boy, there was something distinctly unruly about him. Maybe it was the way his bright eyes darted about and his lips mumbled a constant string of questions. The child was scratching at the rebellious mop of hair on his head, which had been wrestled down with copious amounts of grease. As for the woman, she was unlike anyone the mirror had ever reflected. She had greenish skin and dark hair, fashioned in an unsettlingly exact haircut.

"Leave us," the bearded man barked to the servants, after they placed the mirror in the middle of the candle-lit room.

The servants complied with much unctuous grovelling, before pulling the door shut behind them.

"Child," commanded the woman, her voice like a hiss. "Go to the mirror."

"Why?" asked the boy. "What are we doing?"

"Do not question her, Bijan," snapped the man. His words were accompanied by a raised hand. The threat of it was enough to persuade the boy to do as he was told.

The child sat a few feet from the base of the mirror, fidgeting with the hem of his shirt, unruly locks drooping over his eyes.

"After, can I go outside and play with Anahita?"

"Silence, Bijan!"

Before the man could storm over and strike his son, the woman spoke.

"Introduce yourself, child," she said, her voice devoid of emotion.

The boy grinned a gapped smile. "That's silly."

"Do it!" growled the man, his fury so palpable his eyes were popping.

"Hello, mirror," giggled the child, more amused than scared. "I am Bijan."

The boy's playful words hung in the silence that followed. Suddenly, the woman hissed and snatched at the air with unnatural speed. There was a subtle darkening around the chamber. The candles dimmed. The room grew cold. As if drawn with a hot poker, crimson letters appeared carved in mid-space, hovering before the shocked faces of the father and his young son.

B I J A N

The boy gasped in fear. The man held his breath. The woman remained perfectly still, her unblinking stare gleaming in the red light.

"Bijan to Najib," she whispered. "Najib to Bijan."

The letters shifted and reformed.

NAJIB

In that moment, there was a suffocated rasping sound, like someone being strangled. The mirror had witnessed its fair share of assassinations. This was a royal palace, after all. Tendrils of swaying black energy began to pour from the boy's mouth, ears, and eyes. His face twisted in pain. An expression so horrifying, the mirror doubted it had ever reflected back such suffering. Then, just as quickly, it was over. The candles burned brighter. The name carved in mid-air dissipated.

The boy looked at himself in the mirror, the fear he'd worn a moment earlier melted away into a look of calm contemplation.

The mirror reflected back his differences. The boy's nose was smaller and straighter, his curly hair tamed, his full cheeks thinned, and his eager, inquisitive eyes stilled in an expression of quiet purpose. But there was something else too. The child was drained of some ineffable quality that had made him "the boy".

"Did it work?" the man asked sternly.

"We will see," replied the woman. She turned her attention to the child with a sharp snap of her head. "Speak, Bijan. You wished to go outside and play. Now what do you wish to do?"

"I want to serve Sipera and bring glory to my father's name."

For the first time, the man's visage softened into an almost gratified expression.

The mirror did not understand why. After all, the boy was broken now. When the mirror caught Bijan's reflection in itself, it did not feel quite right. To be honest, the mirror wasn't feeling like itself either…

"What happened to the mirror?" asked the man, a trace of concern in his tone.

The mirror was wondering that too. It felt taller, a little more three-dimensional. Insofar as having hands, feet, and a head.

"What is your name?" asked the woman, coming up to it.

All at once, the mirror distinctly remembered the moment everything had changed. For the worse.

"I am Najib."

It was the strangest feeling the mirror had ever experienced. The first feeling, in fact.

The stern man frowned at the sound of Najib's scratchy voice.

"Not particularly lifelike."

"Its speech is limited to three words at most, but it will be enough to appear human," replied the woman. "If people start asking questions, execute them. They will soon keep their questions to themselves." She paused. "The two servants who brought the mirror here. Start with them."

The man nodded slowly. "It will be done."

"As for the changes in the boy." The woman's lips pursed as if she'd bitten into something acidic. "Say to those who ask that it was a blessing from the goddess Radia, a deity dear to your people. No one questions their gods."

She spoke the word "gods" in a tone verging on disdain. Obviously, the woman did not have much time for the divine.

The man nodded again at this. "A convincing tale."

"I am Najib," repeated Najib, feeling it was somewhat pertinent.

After that troubling day, the mirror's new existence began. It became Najib. An ambling case of metal with the dual purpose of being a vessel for evil and a tool for good. One that never left the boy's side. Things would only go back to some semblance of normality at night, when Najib became an *aayne* again, and the boy would gaze into its reflective surface and pray in hushed whispers that all his wickedness be transferred from him to Najib. And as these opposing forces of light and dark within the boy were forcefully separated, new urges began to emerge from Najib. To right wrongs. To bring justice. Najib watched as, year by year, the boy grew, filling an armour of his own. And how Bijan was becoming a bit like a mirror himself. A mirror of what others wanted him to be.

While it had not been pleasant to be heated to an untold temperature by the blazing fireball, Najib had to admit it was better to be a mirror again. Less problematic. You show people what they are. Not what they would want to be.

"Please… Please help me, Najib."

Ah. There it was. The face Najib knew best. That of the little boy from long ago. It seemed fitting that Bijan would be the last person Najib would ever mirror, before grime and blood would forever take the shine from its surface. This time, Najib did not take anything from the man. It just did what it was always meant to do.

The boy screamed. And laughed. And cried quite a lot. He did not accept this.

But Najib did not care. It was a mirror. And Bijan was himself.

The universe finally made sense.

There was a kind of darkness in the depths beneath Lighthelm Cathedral, unlike any Bijan had ever experienced. A darkness so impenetrable and relentless it was as if his eyes were coated in tar, his drumming heart the only hint that he still existed somewhere within it.

Bijan was not sure he could have escaped such a place. A part of him wished he might not. If he never emerged from the bowels of the earth, certain messy affairs may be easily settled. His father would think his son had died fighting the demon. No doubt, the last male heir and champion of the All-good Radia would be celebrated with much pomp and ceremony, before being placed in his allocated slot in the royal catacombs and shelved like a dull old book. No one would miss him. Aside from his sister, perhaps. The name Emir Bijan Al-Malek would be like another granule of sand in the barren desert of his homeland, forgotten and forgettable – for he would never be his father's worthy successor.

On a positive note, there would be no more expectations. No more tests. No more burdens for him to carry. To find a way out of this pestilent black hole meant continuing to live. And Bijan was not sure he could do that. Not without Najib.

Finally, after what felt like hours of ambling blindly about the demonic abyss, Bijan's hands had found a steepening cavity in the wall which angled its way upwards. The soft, grainy dirt squeezed between the gaps in his fingers, as he crawled on his knees up the slippery tunnel. Halfway up, Bijan ripped his breastplate off his chest and the pauldrons and greaves from his limbs, shedding the cumbersome pieces of armour as he dragged himself through the muck.

Just a day or so ago, Bijan's intent had been steely and his determination unwavering. Nothing could tire him. Nothing could hurt him. Pain was for the weak and surrender for the cowardly. Now, the aches in his body and the collection of bruises and abrasions he'd gathered during his recent fight with Sha-sha chipped away at his resolve. Najib had been the receptacle of all his doubts and weaknesses. Without the *aayne*, there was nowhere else for them to go. It was just him. And he was not enough.

Then, as if from a dream, there was light.

Bijan emerged from the void and into Lighthelm Cathedral's vast hall. He slumped on the rubble, gaping up at the partly collapsed ceiling. The glimpse of the moon through the cracks in the vaults startled him. He had to remind himself they had won. The demon of Elderstay had been vanquished. The horrid yellow barrier was no more. The corpses of the dead lay inert in the streets, at peace at last. He almost envied them.

Bijan would have expected to feel some small elation at this victory. After all, it was to be his final test. To vanquish a demon in Radia's name and prove his worth to his father.

Except, it was not you who killed the demon, was it?

A sneering voice in the back of his mind. One of many.

Bijan swallowed hard. There had been no voices when Najib was with him. Yet there was truth in those words. He felt the frigid touch of the night on his clammy skin. Breathing the icy air was like swallowing shards of glass. He had surfaced from the monster's lair a lesser man. A man full of demons. Demons in his hair. Demons in his belly. Demons scratching at his flesh, pumping his veins with dread. A battle was tearing him up inside, one he could not win.

"Not without Najib."

Bijan rose unsteadily to his feet and staggered towards the cathedral's open doors. The magical forcefield, which had barred his way at the entrance when he'd first attempted to pursue the fleeing Gerome and Polly, was gone. He recalled Sha-sha had made him drink the black water from the fountain, adamant it was the only way they might pass unharmed through the spell around Lighthelm Cathedral. At the time, Bijan had questioned her.

"This can't be water. What is it?"

"It is the blood of the demon. We must drink to enter the demon's domain."

"Demon's blood…" He had hesitated, the black liquid at his lips. "Where will all that evil go, now that Najib has been destroyed?"

Sha-sha had not replied. A dull resentment throbbed in Bijan's mind at the thought of the snake woman. Not at her betrayal. At what she had done to him, all those years ago. What his father had done…

The champion found himself hobbling as fast as his stiff legs would carry him, past the fountain and into the mosaicked plaza. His eyes caught a shimmering on the ground, flecks of silver in the moonlight. The broken remains of his "brother". Bijan dropped to his knees, his fingers moving with feverish anguish, plucking the reflective shards from the gaps between the coloured tiles. During the day, Najib was a towering steel armour. Now, in the black of night, Najib had returned to its true form: an *aayne*. A mirror.

Bijan poked the pieces around his palm, catching his own reflection in one of the larger fragments.

"Please," he begged the shards in his hands. "Please help me, Najib."

Bijan's heart lurched. One side of his face appeared to have curled into a lopsided grin. The other was bent in a grimace. Slowly, his features morphed into a silent scream. Then, as he felt the cry might burst from him with the strength of a thunder crack, he exploded into childish laughter. Gazing in terror at his shifting reflection, Bijan felt a sudden painful stab of heat, no larger than a coin, against his chest. The amulet. The one that detected evil.

"No…" he whispered. "No! NO!"

He squeezed the fragments so tight he bled, begging them to take back all his insecurities and wickedness. The voices he'd been trying to suppress, to smother, to stave off, clawed their way to the surface of his mind.

This is all the gnome's fault! I should have cut him down!

No, Gerome freed me. He helped me!

Shattered me! Broke me!

I need Najib!

Tears flowed from his eyes. Pain and release. Gratitude and hatred. Despair and joy. Confusion. Resentment. Liberation. Everything that was bad and everything that was good, all at once. Najib had been a dam against the river of darkness within him. With Najib gone, Bijan's blackest thoughts might sweep him away. He would be lost to himself. The prince he was meant to be. The would-be ruler of Sipera. Drowned.

There was only one way his father would ever accept his disgrace.

"Kill a demon," the Sultan had commanded. "If you succeed in this final quest, you will be my worthy successor, Bijan Al-Malek."

The seed of a plan quickened in Bijan's fractured mind.

The demon of Elderstay is destroyed. I can tell everyone I did it.

But this notion was cast aside, just as swiftly.

It wasn't me who killed the demon. Others will claim the victory. Sipera will find out. My father will find out. Even if he doesn't, I'll know.

Another idea. One far more feasible.

Kill Gerome, then. He's a demon.

Hesitation.

No, Gerome is my… friend.

Truth.

A friend would not have left me here. Broken. Like this.

The mirror's fragments slipped from Bijan's hands, red with his blood. Through gritted teeth, he smiled. A smile both gleeful and vexed as the world came into focus, a knitted mess of contradictions he'd need a lifetime to unravel.

His shattered thoughts seemed to agree on one thing.

"Gerome," he breathed, the name spoken like an oath to the glistening shards in the night. "I'm coming for you."

The chilly air nipped at Brent's nose as he rocked atop the white steed – a magnificent beast the Lord of Snowden-slash-Elderstay hadn't gotten around to naming. The horse probably had possessed some foreign-sounding Siperan moniker. Brent intended to duly rename the creature something more befitting its new status. Maybe "Carrier of Nobility", or "Burdened with Greatness". The champions' horses belonged to Brent now. As did any property left behind by its former owners, if they did not show up to reclaim it within three working days, as per the small print on their recruitment letters.

Brent grinned lukewarmly at the thought of the "people of talent" he'd been made to hire. It was a relief that only *one* had returned.

That gnome son of a bitch. Gerome. Gerome the gnome. Such a silly name.

He dwelled sadly upon Snowden's coffers. His accountant had been quick to point out they were well-nigh empty. Brent could not afford any more heroes returning from this mission. If he found any more of his former recruits along the way, he would be sure to – erm – *reward* them for their efforts. By nudging them off a cliff.

His mind touched on the interchangeable Siperan champions, the well-meaning and gullible brothers, Bijan and Najib. He couldn't quite remember who was who. Then there was the girl, Polly. Same name as his niece, Edmund's daughter, who had died during the fall of Elderstay. Funny coincidence. More hesitantly, Brent's thoughts lingered on Sha-sha.

The snake woman had assured him she would be the only one to return. *Can't keep your word if you're dead.* Truth be told, she wouldn't be missed. Sha-sha had given Brent the creeps. Yet had it not been for her, he would not be travelling to Elderstay at this very moment, a song in his heart. Sha-sha had appeared at the gates of Snowden one night, claiming to know a hex that could lift the demon barrier around his brother's cursed city. Brent had not wanted to believe her at first. Thought her a scammer and a charlatan. He'd almost had her shot by his sentries. But Sha-sha had demanded no recompense, other than the wish to speak with him about a plan to reclaim Elderstay. Best of all, the woman had said she did not want monetary rewards, nor did she care much for titles and land, either. Sha-sha said there was something within Elderstay itself that she desired. Brent had gawked at such a generous offer. And given he'd assumed Elderstay and all its contents lost to him, there was no harm in allowing the strange woman to take what she pleased, as long as the demon was eliminated and Elderstay returned to him.

It was for the best that she was gone for good.

Brent surveyed the men walking in single file ahead of him and found the solemn crunching of boots on the frozen ground and the banner whipping about in the breeze invigorating. The bronze helmet between crossed swords. The insignia of the House of Agris. *His* House – as the oldest living male – Brent reminded himself smugly. A symbol of strength and divine right. An image he was keen to restore in the minds of allies and foes alike.

Lord Brent casually cast his eyes upon the frosted planes, the icy hardened vegetation, and the caves that tunnelled through the rocky landscape in the distance, closest to the mountain peaks. Home to the Nord-ul goblins – *for now*. He was going to be making changes around here. Relocating the goblin rabble would be top priority. Any encroaching would be severely punished. Lighting a few fires at the entrance of their dens should convince them to move on. Goblins were not the types to put up much of a fight.

His lips twisted beneath his bushy beard. It was common knowledge among those inclined to make such comparisons that Snowden was little more than an outpost to the northern territories. A pinprick before the sprawling Shiver Expanse, and a meagre offcut from his late father's vast domain. For a long time, Brent had made do with scraps.

Elderstay had been the jewel of the House of Agris – little over a decade prior, one of the most powerful noble families in Tellarin. Had Father entrusted the care of Elderstay to him, they still would be. Yet Father had been narrow in vision. Entrusting to Edmund, the eldest of his two sons, all that was worth having. Elderstay, a wealthy Xeranta wife, the fabled Lighthelm. To Brent, Snowden and its pretence of a reward, when it was no more than a punishment…

"Elderstay ahead!" called a voice from the lead soldiers.

Then, a few moments later, "What's going on? What is that?"

A panicked cacophony of mutters and gasps rose from the ranks.

Brent felt his horse stir beneath him. A whirlwind of polychromatic dust was rising over Elderstay. It was like a living thing, swirling above the city and swarming about the walls and parapets. Brent gazed in horror as huge growths began to appear where the dust was thickest.

"That deceitful dog!" he spat, feeling a sudden urge to unsheathe his sword. "Gerome said they had vanquished the demon!"

"Lord Brent," stammered one of the soldiers closest to him, a slight unease in his tone. "This looks nothing like the demonic barrier. It's… it's something else."

"What is it, then?"

The soldier tilted his head slightly to one side.

"Could be a mushroom, Your Lordship."

Polly stood on the vast balcony of what had once been the best view in Elderstay. Her sprawling family mansion once overlooked the lavish gardens, the busy cobblestone streets, and the ornate mosaic patterns in the town squares that had coloured her childhood with a sense of wonder. The deserted and demeaned Elderstay lay prone before her, ready for a new ruler to lift it from its knees. Her eyes rose over the city to the mountains that surrounded Elderstay from all around, creating an almost impregnable curtain of white peaks. She watched as ant-like dots approached the steep ravine, nearing the stone bridge that connected Elderstay to the rest of the world.

Polly smiled to herself. "Hello, Uncle Brent."

She stepped back into the foyer that backed onto the large, vaulted hall. As she did so, her gaze turned instinctively to the small pile of rounded stones she'd gathered beneath a large family portrait of the late Lord and Lady of Elderstay.

"Hey, little brother," she murmured, addressing the mound of smoothed rocks, her voice dropping to a gentle whisper as she approached the child's grave.

She kneeled in silence for a time, her solemn thoughts like sharp barbs in her mind. Regret for what might have been. Grief for what had happened. She allowed herself to feel it all, eleven years of wandering like an exile, eleven years of guilt for being the only survivor of the rulers of Elderstay.

"I never got to know you. We never got to play together, argue, or make up. I never got to see you grow to be the Lord of Elderstay. To inherit the Lighthelm. We'll never know if I'd be jealous. If you'd turn out to be a little brat. If we'd be friends despite it all... I'm sorry."

Polly felt her throat tighten as she spoke. Her eyes travelled upwards to the family portrait that hung on the wall, blemished and torn in places, yet whole enough to make out her parents' faces. The visages of her father,

Lord Edmund, her mother, Lady Desta, and a younger version of herself nestled between them stared back at her, stoic and unsmiling, as befitted the depictions of nobles. In a flash of remembrance, she recalled the day her father had commissioned that painting. How bored she'd been, how her frizzy hair had to be repeatedly tucked back behind her ears by her mother every time she squirmed restlessly. A memory from another life.

"Mum, Dad, I will be the Lady of Elderstay now. I am sorry you can't be here too. But I wanted you to know I am home. And I will take care of everything."

Polly rose with purpose and stepped inside the hall. The sprawling room had once been decorated with vivid depictions of the House of Agris' history and holy imagery. The ancient god who'd gifted her ancestor the Lighthelm had looked over this place, depicted as an orb of light painted on every wall, along with sacred symbols etched in the old tongue on the archways and surviving pillars. The frescoes were now fading and cracked. The hall was littered with rubble, a decade of dirt, and a handful of dead bodies. Never mind. It would all be fine in a minute.

Polly strode up to her father's piano. She'd found the polished wooden exterior blanketed beneath a layer of fine dust, bearing the scars of time and neglect. Not far from the piano, she'd retrieved the chipped and rickety wooden stool her father would sit on when the mood took him. He'd been an unexpectedly creative man with more the tender heart of an artist than the pragmatic mind of a leader.

Polly eased herself on the stool, the way her father would. The piano was a bit tall for her. A plush mushroom appeared beneath her feet. Better.

She tapped on one of the dulled ivory keys. A forlorn note rang in the hall, breaking the deathly silence the demon had left in its wake. Chubby growths appeared where Polly's fingers had rapped against the ivories.

"Ready, Mushy?" she asked, addressing the invisible presence that shared her being.

A rush in her blood confirmed they were. Polly closed her eyes and allowed her Leshi to see the world as she envisioned it. To dig deep into her imagination, the subtle shapes and colours in her dreams, the memories of what was once her home. Vibrant. Alive. Beautiful. As it had been, before the demon had taken Elderstay from her.

The melody swelled under Polly's hands. The music flowed like a fluid, filling every inch of the hall and seeping into the stone walls, travelling down into the earth beneath the city.

A veining of coppery tendrils slivered down her seat and seeped into the grooves in the floor. Budding along the cracks in the stonework, mushrooms moulded themselves around every bare surface, scaling the walls and ceiling until everything was a forest of variegated, rounded growths. The mushrooms broke open and a gale of spores whirled about the hall, before pouring down the balcony like a waterfall of dust. The mist rushed through the alleyways and streets, seeking the darkest corners and the widest plazas, entering the doors and windows and lying softly on the inert bodies of Elderstay's long-dead inhabitants. All of it, from the lowest basement to the tip of the tallest tower, became covered in a thick layer of lichen and moss. Soon, Polly felt Mushy rise airborne, enjoying the height, spreading all over the empty city in a cloud of new life, swaying with the music.

"This is our home," whispered the spores in the wind.

Polly smiled, her fingers dancing along the piano keys.

"Yes, Mushy, this is *our* home."

right, weren't you supposed to be off tomorrow? To Maracanda?"

"Pointless. All pointless. I mean. The docks are still under quara… quara…"

"Under what?"

"The docks are closed! The quara-n-tine!" I repeated with what I believed to be the eloquence of the most gifted speaker in Grandfall.

"Oh, the *quarantine*. Hasn't the Magusterium sorted that one out yet?" Partridge absentmindedly handed me back the receipt and resumed wiping down the counter, more for show than hygienic purposes. "You should go to bed, Gerome."

My friend's tone suggested disappointment at the prospect I wouldn't embark on a perilous journey to someplace remote and inhospitable any time soon. But all I heard, in the midst of my drunken stupor, was that I was going to be denied another drink. This upset me greatly.

"You're not my mother, Partridge. Not. My. *Moth – er.*"

My threatening finger swayed in front of my nose. Then the world swayed with it. I felt my head drop forward like an anvil, while the rest of me slipped into a warm, sloshing fluid. I sank in the feeling as if it were a bath. A bath of pleasant nothingness in which I could drown all my worries…

I am not certain for how long I was out. The wicked white wine blotted out pretty much everything, from the moment Partridge denied me to the moment I woke. Mid fall. When my stool was whisked from underneath me.

I hit the floor hard. Dots of light burst across my vision as my eyes flew open. And there I was. Flat on my back. Rushing feet stampeding all around me. People were screaming. I recognised Partridge's high-pitched wails.

"What the hell…?" I lifted myself up, rubbing my head.

The *Roaring Peacock* was a battlefield. Tables and chairs had been overturned. Most of the patrons had vacated or were spectating from behind makeshift barricades. Broken glasses and bottles mantled the floor in shards and sticky puddles.

I blinked at the bizarre scene.

The trendy establishment and, currently, my home address was – unbeknown to its innkeeper – a gathering place for men of certain wayward inclinations. Hence, bar fights were not frequent. We found other ways to release pent-up aggression. In more private settings. With candles and whipped cream.

"Come at me, you pointy-eared pricks!"

Through blurred vision, I spotted an elderly man. He had clambered on a table in the middle of the *Roaring Peacock,* his fists curled up belligerently. His thick bushy beard was so long it stroked his knees and vaguely covered his–

Oh.

He was naked.